Savannah Spectator

Blind Item

If you think Savannah's newest elected official was done shocking us now that the campaign is over, you have another think coming! His recent public appearances with his ex-campaign manager, a lovely young woman twenty years his junior, have caused more than a few tongues to wag. Their words may claim, "Just business," but their body language screams, "Hot, hot, hot"!

But what's this? If her recent purchases (baby clothes, books on childbirth) are any indication, it seems we are in for a double shock, dear readers—unless Ms. Campaign Manager is keeping her condition a secret, it may just be our elected official who gets the shock of his life this time!

Dear Reader,

Welcome to another stellar month of smart, sensual reads. Our bestselling series DYNASTIES: THE DANFORTHS comes to a compelling conclusion with Leanne Banks's *Shocking the Senator* as honest Abe Danforth finally gets his story. Be sure to look for the start of our next family dynasty story when Eileen Wilks launches DYNASTIES: THE ASHTONS next month and brings you all the romance and intrigue you could ever desire…all set in the fabulous Napa Valley.

Award-winning author Jennifer Greene is back this month to conclude THE SCENT OF LAVENDER series with the astounding *Wild in the Moment*. And just as the year brings some things to a close, new excitement blossoms as Alexandra Sellers gives us the next installment of her SONS OF THE DESERT series with *The Ice Maiden's Sheikh*. The always-enjoyable Emilie Rose will wow you with her tale of *Forbidden Passion*—let's just say the book starts with a sexy tryst on a staircase. We'll let you imagine the rest. Brenda Jackson is also back this month with her unforgettable hero Storm Westmoreland, in *Riding the Storm*. (A title that should make you go hmmm.) And rounding things out is up-and-coming author Michelle Celmer's second book, *The Seduction Request*.

I would love to hear what you think about Silhouette Desire, so please feel free to drop me a line c/o Silhouette Books, 233 Broadway, Suite 1001, New York, NY 10279. Let me know what miniseries you are enjoying, your favorite authors and things you would like to see in the future.

With thanks,

Melissa Jeglinski

Melissa Jeglinski
Senior Editor
Silhouette Desire

Please address questions and book requests to:
Silhouette Reader Service
U.S.: 3010 Walden Ave., P.O. Box 1325, Buffalo, NY 14269
Canadian: P.O. Box 609, Fort Erie, Ont. L2A 5X3

SHOCKING
THE SENATOR
LEANNE BANKS

Silhouette®

Desire

Published by Silhouette Books
America's Publisher of Contemporary Romance

Special thanks and acknowledgment are given
to Leanne Banks for her contribution to the
DYNASTIES: THE DANFORTHS series.

SILHOUETTE BOOKS

ISBN 0-373-76621-1

SHOCKING THE SENATOR

Copyright © 2004 by Harlequin Books S.A.

Visit Silhouette Books at www.eHarlequin.com

Printed in U.S.A.

LEANNE BANKS,

a *USA TODAY* bestselling author of romance and 2002 winner of the prestigious Booksellers' Best Award, lives in her native Virginia with her husband, son and daughter. Recognized for both her sensual and humorous writing with two Career Achievement Awards from *Romantic Times*, Leanne likes creating a story with a few grins, a generous kick of sensuality and characters that hang around after the book is finished. Leanne believes romance readers are the best readers in the world because they understand that love is the greatest miracle of all. Contact Leanne online at leannebbb@aol.com or write to her at P.O. Box 1442, Midlothian, VA 23113. An SASE for a reply would be greatly appreciated.

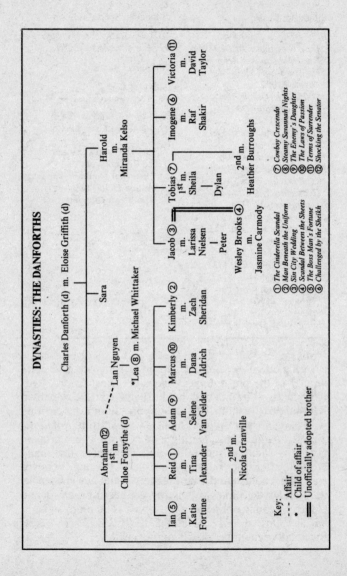

DYNASTIES: THE DANFORTHS

Charles Danforth (d) m. Eloise Griffith (d)

Sara

Harold
m.
Miranda Kelso

Abraham ⑫
1st m.
Chloe Forsythe (d)
----Lan Nguyen
*Lea ⑧ m. Michael Whittaker

2nd m.
Nicola Granville

Ian ⑤
m.
Katie
Fortune

Reid ①
m.
Tina
Alexander

Adam ⑨
m.
Selene
Van Gelder

Marcus ⑩
m.
Dana
Aldrich

Kimberly ②
m.
Zach
Sheridan

Jacob ③
m.
Larissa
Nielsen

Peter

Wesley Brooks ④
m.
Jasmine Carmody

Tobias ⑦
1st m.
Sheila

Dylan

2nd m.
Heather Burroughs

Imogene ⑥
m.
Raf
Shakir

Victoria ⑪
m.
David
Taylor

① *The Cinderella Scandal*
② *Man Beneath the Uniform*
③ *Sin City Wedding*
④ *Scandal Between the Sheets*
⑤ *The Boss Man's Fortune*
⑥ *Challenged by the Sheikh*
⑦ *Cowboy Crescendo*
⑧ *Steamy Savannah Nights*
⑨ *The Enemy's Daughter*
⑩ *The Laws of Passion*
⑪ *Terms of Surrender*
⑫ *Shocking the Senator*

Key:
- - - Affair
* Child of affair
═══ Unofficially adopted brother

Prologue

This man was one big no-no, but Nicola Granville was having a tough time saying anything but yes.

"We said we weren't going to do this anymore," Nicola said as she reluctantly dragged her lips away from Abraham Danforth's firm mouth. With her back against his cold office door, Abe's body felt deliciously warm and strong against hers.

He slid his hands over her hips and pulled her against him. "The election's over, Nic. I won. Why fight it anymore?"

She could name several big reasons, one from her past, which would knock the mighty Abe Danforth, former Navy SEAL, CEO and newly elected senator, right on his surprisingly rock-hard rear end. Abe had turned out to be a surprise to her in many ways. Not many fifty-five-year-old men still had a body that could make most women look twice.

Nicola tried to shake off the familiar melting sensation in her body and brain. "It still wouldn't look right for you to be having an affair with your campaign manager. I'm an expert on these things. After all we've been through, you should know that by now."

"I know you've taken what could have been egg on my face and made everything sunny-side up. Who else could handle a candidate with a beautiful, but illegitimate, daughter that comes out of my past? A son falsely accused of criminal involvement? Who else—"

Shaking her head, Nicola covered his mouth with her hand. "Don't go humble on me now. Your family may have presented some unusual situations for me to manage, but the kind of man you are made my job a lot easier than it could have been. You're the real deal, Abe Danforth. *That's* why you were elected."

"I refuse to argue about this. I know you helped me get elected. But there's always been more between us, even from the beginning."

Nicola felt the addictive sizzle as she stared into Abe's blue eyes. Sometimes she felt as if looking into his eyes was like looking at the sun too long. If she wasn't careful, she would become blinded, in this case to reality.

She closed her eyes, still too aware of his scent and

strength. "I told you I'm not going to Washington with you."

"But you promised you would stay with me during the transition until I'm sworn in," he reminded her, brushing a lock of hair from her cheek.

Nicola opened her eyes. His tenderness made her ache. "Yes, I did," she said, suspecting this would be one of the hardest promises she'd ever had to keep.

"So I have time to change your mind."

"Don't count on it." She wasn't trying to issue a challenge, just the truth.

"Oh, but I am." He slid his leg between her thighs and an image of the intimacy they'd shared taunted her.

Nicola bit her lip and pushed against his chest. "We agreed we wouldn't do this anymore. It was a mistake for us to—" she broke off and swallowed "—get involved this way."

He studied her for a long moment. "Are you saying you regret it?"

No. Yes. No. Yes. "Abe, we've been through this. I don't want what you and I have worked so hard to accomplish to be tainted because—"

"Because what? Because I'm so much older than you are?"

Nicola rolled her eyes. "That's not it and you know it."

"Maybe," he said, clearly not convinced. "I'm almost twenty years older than you."

"Your body sure doesn't seem like it," she muttered

under her breath. She never ceased to be amazed by his stamina in and out of bed. She shook her head. "I'm not going to let you talk circles around me. Even though the election is over, it's still my job to make the best public relations choices for you and, trust me, I would be your worst PR nightmare yet."

"I have a hard time connecting the word nightmare with you, Nic," he murmured, trailing his fingers down her cheek and throat to the top of her breast.

Her heart pounded in her chest at the expression of wanting on his face. The combination of his strength and need for her never failed to turn her protests to dust. He was so strong. How could he want her so much? How could she refuse him? He made her feel things she'd never thought she could feel. She tried to steel herself against him, but her bones and resistance turned to water.

"You don't like the way I touch you," he said, dipping his finger lower, just glancing her nipple and making her shudder.

She bit her lip. "You know that's not true," she whispered.

"You don't like the way I kiss you," he said, lowering his mouth to hers again and making her dizzy.

Not fair, her puny rational side wanted to cry, but the rest of her was sinking into the delicious, decadent, forbidden pleasure of Abe.

"You don't like the way I make love to you," he murmured against her mouth as he skimmed his hands down to the waistband of her dress slacks and unfastened them.

This was the time to say no, a faint voice inside her coached her.

The sound of her zipper lowering mingled with his breath and hers. Nicola knew what was coming if she didn't stop him. She knew he would touch her size ten body and make her feel as if she was the most beautiful, sexiest woman in the world. He would caress her gently, paying attention to her response. He would guide her hands over him and allow her to make him sweat, just a little. Making him sweat, however, only made her hotter and more restless until he took her over the edge and sank inside her.

"I want you, Nicola," he said in a rough, sexy voice that had the same affect as an intimate stroke in her secret places.

Mentally swearing, she surrendered. One more time, she told herself. Just one more time.

One

Two pink lines on the at-home pregnancy test.

Two pink lines on the second at-home pregnancy test.

Panic slammed through her. Nicola couldn't believe her eyes. Sure, she'd missed her last period, but she'd never been particularly regular. Plus, she was thirty-seven years old and all the recent data suggested that a woman's fertility started going down the tubes by the time she turned twenty-six.

The second missed period and the lingering nausea had made her nervous enough to do the drugstore pregnancy test. Inside the bathroom of her large temporary suite in Crofthaven, she stared at the twin positive results for a full moment.

How could you have been so stupid? Didn't you learn your lesson the first time?

Nicola closed her eyes at the stab from her ruthless conscience. A hundred emotions rumbled inside her like a volcano that had been silent for years. She couldn't help remembering the other time in her life when she'd gotten pregnant.

No one close to her had seemed to be able to look her in the eye. Her foster parents had been utterly humiliated. Her high school boyfriend had insisted he was too young to be a father.

The only person who had looked at her without condemnation had been the woman at the home for unwed mothers.

Nicola's stomach knotted at the memory. She'd felt so trapped and frightened. She hadn't known where to turn. She'd been unable to go through with an abortion, yet every day the truth hit her in the face that she didn't have the resources to take care of a baby.

So she'd carried her baby for nine months and given her away. Her chest began to ache with a terrible pain she'd felt throughout the years. *Don't go there,* she told herself. "She has wonderful parents who love her with all their hearts. It was the right decision. It was the best thing for her." She said it aloud to drown out her regrets.

But Nicola had never totally gotten past the feeling that she must have been a bad person to give up her child.

She bit her lip and opened her eyes, the test results shouting at her. *How could you be so stupid? Twice!*

"Where's Nicola?" Abraham asked his housekeeper, Joyce, as she delivered his morning breakfast on a tray. He noted the tray only held one plate with an omelette and toast, one glass of orange juice and one cup of coffee. Nicola usually took her breakfast with him. He enjoyed starting his morning with her. No matter what crisis the day promised, she made him feel lighter.

"Miss Granville said she's not feeling well this morning. She sends her regrets."

Abraham frowned. Her regrets? She could have spoken to him directly.

The housekeeper must have noticed his displeasure. "She said her stomach was bothering her." She paused then added, "It may be cramps, her, uh, lady's time and she was uncomfortable—"

Abe gave a short nod, surprised that Nicola would be uncomfortable discussing anything with him. They'd been as close as a man and woman could get physically, mentally…maybe even emotionally.

He took a sip of his coffee. "Thank you, Joyce. It looks perfect, as usual."

His housekeeper beamed from the praise. "You're welcome, sir. Let me know if you want anything else."

"How are you doing?" he asked, silently referring to her grief over her daughter's death.

"Thank you for asking. Every day it gets a little better," she said and left the room.

His son Marcus poked his head through the door. "Good morning. How's the progress on your move to Washington?"

"Progressing," Abe grumbled, frowning at the boxes of files and papers occupying a quarter of his large office.

"You don't look happy at the moment, Senator-elect," Marcus said.

Abe gave a short chuckle and met his son's gaze. There was a slight easing of tension in his relationship with Marc, although Abe still sensed a guarded wariness from his son. When Marc had been framed, then ultimately cleared, of a crime he didn't commit, Abe had been outraged. Nicola had helped him see Marc in a different way. He was proud of Marc's strength and ingenuity and damn glad he'd found a good woman. Abe knew Marc still didn't understand all the choices Abe had made when the children were young, but his son didn't seem to be as resentful as he had been in the past.

"I'm trying to figure out how to persuade Nicola to come to Washington to manage my staff," Abe confessed.

Marcus raised his eyebrows in surprise. "I didn't know she wasn't going. You two have worked together so well."

"Yes, we have, but she insists that she'd rather stay in Georgia."

"She's probably got her pick of offers. Nothing like

being on the winning team to boost your career, especially in her business."

"True," Abe said, rubbing his chin thoughtfully. "Maybe I just haven't come up with the right combination of terms."

"If anyone can persuade her, you can," Marc said.

"Thanks for the vote of confidence. How's your FBI agent wife?"

"Working hard. We're close to getting evidence on the people who tried to frame me. She says it's personal." Marc shook his head. "Pretty amazing woman that dropped into my life. Can't get more lucky than that."

Abe saw Marc's love for his new wife shining from his eyes. "It's good having you here for the holidays."

"It's good being here. Different than usual. You seem different," Marc said. "Less tense. I guess winning the election helped."

"Yes, it did." It was odd as hell, but now that the battle was over, he was left feeling empty. The exhilaration of the win had faded. He was looking forward to the challenge of serving in Congress. He felt as if it was his duty, his destiny, but the campaign had put stress on his family. In watching his sons and daughter meeting every challenge, Abe was more aware than ever of all he had missed during their growing-up years.

"You and your brothers and sister showed what you were made of during the campaign. Lord knows I wasn't there for you when you were growing up." He tasted the bitter, familiar flavor of regret. "I can't take credit for how you've turned out, but I'm proud of all of you."

Surprise crossed Marc's face. "That's the first time I've heard you say that."

"It's not the first time I've thought it," Abe said gruffly, reminded again of his less-than-stellar performance as a father and a husband.

"Mom always said you had more important things to do than be here with us."

Anger rushed through him, but he bit his tongue. Abe didn't want to speak poorly of his late wife. He had never been able to please her. "She was right in a way. I needed to prove myself. Your mother and I didn't have a perfect marriage. We wanted different things."

"What things?"

"She didn't want to be married to a military man. She didn't want to leave Savannah and Crofthaven."

"Weren't you in the military when you two got married?" Marc seemed to want to get his questions answered while he had the chance.

Abe nodded. "Yes, but she thought she could change me." He held up his hand when Marc looked as if he wanted to ask another question. "Listen, your mother loved all of you and she wanted the best for you. I won't disrespect her memory. She doesn't deserve that. I stand by my choices, good and bad."

Abe saw a hint of vulnerability cross his son's face that cut him to the quick. A glimpse of the hurt Marc had endured because Abe had been too busy fighting his own demons to be a dad. Excuses, he thought. He didn't believe in making excuses. There was nothing else to say.

Marc gave a shrug. "I'll let you get back to your packing," he said.

"Marc," Abe said. "You're always welcome."

His son gave a slow nod full of wariness and walked away.

Abe bit back an oath. This was what he deserved. Respect, but distance.

Two hours later, Abe heard a knock at his office door. Nicola appeared and he felt his heart speed up. Crazy fool, he admonished himself. He stood, allowing his gaze to fall over her. He liked the way her red hair bounced over her shoulders as she walked toward him. She wore a black pantsuit that hinted at the curves beneath. She was rounded the way a woman should be, and when she wore heels, she stood tall enough to look him in the eye. He'd never met a woman who'd gotten to him more quickly. "I wondered when you were going to show up."

"Didn't Joyce tell you—"

He nodded, rounding his desk to be closer to her. "Yes, she said something about a stomachache or cramps?"

"Something like that," she said with a shrug.

"Are you better?"

"I'm fine."

He took her hand. "I've been thinking. I really want you in Washington with me. Name your price."

Nicola's eyes rounded and she shook her head. "Wow. Good morning to you, too. I told you I'm going to stay in Savannah."

"You can keep your home in Savannah and stay here when the Senate isn't in session. I can make this very easy for you. Liberal leave. I'll even subsidize your housing in Washington. Think of the contacts you'll make." He squeezed her hand. It felt cool within his. Too cool. "Are you still not feeling well?"

"I'm okay," she said.

"Your hand is cold," he said, and rubbed her palm between his. "You seem distracted."

"I actually have some things I need to take care of this afternoon, so I was going to ask if I could take the rest of the day off."

"Sure," he said, confused by her distant attitude. "Do you need to talk about something?"

She looked away from him. "No, I just need to take care of some errands."

"You know that if you ever need anything, all you have to do is ask me," he told her.

She gave a half-hearted smile. "Of course."

"We can have dinner when you get back."

"I may not be back in time. You'd probably better go ahead without me."

His gut twisted and he tightened his hand around hers. "You know I don't play games, Nic. What's up?"

She bit her lip. "I really do have some things I need to take care of this afternoon. Personal things."

Which she didn't want to share with him. Abe felt a door shut in his face. He shouldn't be bothered. Nicola was younger than he was and he kept telling himself she should find someone closer to her own age…. They were the epitome of consenting adults, and both had fought the flash fire of sexual awareness that simmered between them from the beginning. The emotional connection that developed throughout the campaign had made it nearly impossible not to take her to bed. "Nic, we've been through a lot during the last year. I know I'm not the right man for you in the long run, but I want you to know you can turn to me."

She paled and swallowed audibly. "Thanks," she murmured and walked out of the room.

Thank goodness her gynecologist had agreed to see her immediately. After a couple of tests Nicola sat on the hard examination table and waited. The tests were for the benefit of the doctor. Nicola already knew and accepted the truth. She was pregnant. She was having the baby even if she had to raise him or her on her own. She just didn't know how to tell Abe.

She felt a stab of guilt. This was the kind of thing that could ruin his career, and Nicola, more than anyone, believed Abe Danforth was going to rock Washington D.C.

A knock sounded on the door and her doctor, a kind, no-nonsense woman in her fifties, entered. "Good afternoon, Nicola."

"Good afternoon, Dr. Baxter. Thank you for working me in."

Dr. Baxter nodded and looked at the chart she carried. "You're pregnant. Did you suspect?"

Nicola nodded. "I'm here for the vitamins."

Dr. Baxter glanced at the chart again. "Has your marital status changed?"

Nicola shook her head. "Still single. I'm a big girl. I can take care of me and the baby."

Dr. Baxter met her gaze. "I'm sure you can."

Nicola relaxed a smidgen at the doctor's confidence. She would be okay, especially after this gosh-awful morning sickness passed.

Unable to sleep, Nicola crept into the kitchen after midnight. She'd picked up a variety box of herbal teas at the same time she'd filled the prescription for her prenatal vitamins and hoped a cup would calm her nerves. Bypassing a noisy kettle, she boiled water in a small pan. She pulled a cup from the cabinet, tossed in a bag that promised soothing qualities and poured the hot water over it.

"Can't sleep, either?" Abe asked from the doorway.

Nicola whirled around, her heart climbing into her throat.

"A couple shots of whiskey might work better," he said, lifting a bottle of liquor that she knew cost more than her most expensive shoes. He was dressed in a pair of lounging pants and a nightshirt partially unbuttoned to reveal a muscular chest that belied his age. Nicola liked him best this way, with his hair mussed and his manner casual and approachable.

That was what had gotten her into trouble in the first place, she reminded herself. She cleared her throat. "I want to try this tea. It promises relaxation."

His lips tilted in an engaging grin as he moved toward her. "There are lots of ways to relax. Why are you tense? The election's over, babe."

Nicola turned her attention to her tea. "Oh, you're type-A, so you know how it is. Your mind starts whirling and won't stop. I guess I could ask you why you're awake—" He slid his fingers through her hair to the back of her neck.

"Yeah, you're stiff. What's wrong?"

Her heart hammered from his touch. "I told you," she said. "My mind is whirling."

"About what?" he asked, rubbing his thumb over a knot.

She bit her lip at the soothing sensation. The man was so good with his hands, she thought, and a dozen forbidden images of Abe with his hands on her body slipped through her mind.

"You got quiet. Am I doing something right?"

She cleared her throat. "Too right," she murmured. "You always seem to know exactly how to touch—" She broke off again and couldn't swallow her moan as he found another knot.

She felt him lift her hair and his mouth pressed against her bare skin. "I know a more effective way of taking care of your tension," he murmured, his voice creating a delicious buzz on her neck. He slid his hand around to the front of her and eased her bottom against the front of him.

Nicola closed her eyes. She could feel his arousal. It never ceased to amaze her that he could want her this way. He seemed to have the power to make her forget everything but being with him this very moment. *Maybe things could work out between them.* Unbidden, the hopeful thought squeaked out. Maybe the magic between them could work for something longer. "We've never really talked about the future," she managed to say.

"Yes, we have," he said, rubbing his mouth over her shoulder. "I want you to come to Washington with me."

Caught between arousal and the desire to tell him about the baby, she swallowed hard. "I mean we've never talked about us personally."

He paused. "What do you mean?"

Thankful he couldn't see her face, she inhaled carefully. "I mean our personal future. We've said we shouldn't be involved, but we keep giving in to temptation."

Abe pulled back slightly. "Do you want to go public?"

"Do you?"

His sigh drifted over her hair. "I hadn't thought about it. It was impossible during the campaign. I've liked keeping the personal us just for you and me. Lord knows, the public has the rest of me. I like having you and me just for you and me. I know I'm too old for you for anything long-term."

"What if I disagreed with you on that?" she asked, feeling her chest tighten.

"You'd change your mind when I get arthritis and you're still moving and shaking," he said with a laugh that didn't set right with her. "I don't see any need for me to get married again. I screwed that up pretty well the first time. And having children is the last thing I'd want to do right now. All my children would tell you I was a dismal father figure. I don't want to disappoint another kid because I'm not the father I should be."

But do you want children?

"That's one way you and I are alike, Nic. We both want the freedom to pursue our careers. A marriage and children. You might as well tie an anchor around my neck and toss me in the ocean."

A door to a place inside Nicola that held a tiny ray of light slammed closed. She would go this alone.

* * *

Nicola successfully avoided Abe the entire weekend, but when morning dawned on Monday, she knew she would have to face him, to work with him, and keep her secrets to herself. She only had to last six weeks. Abe would take the oath of office in January. In Washington. Nicola planned a move to the West Coast. A plan of action made all the difference in the world.

Less than six weeks, she told herself and lifted her chin. She pushed Abe's office door the rest of the way open and found him standing with his broad back to her as he stared out the window. His posture was so erect she often wondered if he had a titanium spine.

She stiffened her own shoulders and stole the moment just to look at him. Honest Abe, as the voters knew him, had a killer body and could make her blood run so hot and so fast that her brain just flat-out stopped. His combination of sincerity and strength knocked out her first level of resistance, and the way he looked at her, as if she were the only woman alive, finished off any other defenses she erected.

For all his strength, he looked totally alone. The knowledge bothered her. His children wanted to know him better. He wanted a closer relationship with them. Accomplishing that should be easier, she thought, feeling a familiar trickle of frustration.

Abe turned around and looked at her. "Good morning, Nicola."

His deep voice touched a chord inside her; it always had. Her name felt like beautiful, sensual music coming from his mouth. One more reason she'd found him so difficult to resist. "Good morning to you. How's the packing going?"

"My assistant has grown tired or distracted by the holidays. Her daughter's Christmas program is this morning, so I let her off for the day."

"Nice boss," Nicola said with a smile, moving closer to his desk.

"Misplaced guilt," he corrected in a dry voice. "It made me think of how many of my children's Christmas programs I missed."

"You could do something about your own children."

"Kinda late," he said. "I don't think Marc's interested in making gingerbread men anymore."

Nicola laughed at the image of the two Danforth men up to their elbows in gingerbread cookies and frosting. "I don't think you are, either. I meant you could try to spend some time with each of your children. You could add it to your to-do list before you go to Washington."

"The problem with that is they'll want to ask sticky questions. Marc asked one the other day," he said, leaning against his large cherry desk.

"Questions about what?" she asked, sitting in an upholstered chair and pouring a cup of tea for herself and a cup of coffee for Abe.

"About why I wasn't around more. About his mother."

"Did you tell him the truth?" she asked and took a sip of her tea. Abe had told her about his marriage. His wife had deeply resented his military career and he'd felt unable to please her.

"Some of it." He narrowed his eyes. "She was with the kids more than I was. It wouldn't be fair to disrespect her memory."

Nicola gave a snort of disagreement.

Abe looked at her in surprise. "What?"

"She may have been a wonderful woman, but I don't think she needs to be martyred. Plus, Marc's a big boy. He doesn't need to be protected from the truth. He's a grownup. If he understood more about what made you the poster boy for overachievers, it might actually help him."

"Poster boy for overachievers," Abe echoed, lifting an eyebrow.

Others would be intimidated by that raised eyebrow, but Nicola wasn't. "If there were a man's photo beside the word *overachiever* in the dictionary, it would be yours."

His lips twitched. "I don't know whether to be insulted or complimented. Besides, isn't that like the pot calling the kettle black? You're no slouch."

"I can be lazy," she argued. "I can sleep past 6:00 a.m."

"So can I if I have a good reason," he said, his gaze sliding over her and lingering.

She felt the snap of electricity between them. Yikes,

she would have to be careful. Surprise, surprise. Even though she was pregnant, Abe could still make her too aware of him. "I said sleep, not just stay in bed. But back to your children, I really do think you should add it to your to-do list."

"I'll think about it," he said, and sat across from her. He lifted his coffee to his lips. "Did you take care of your personal matters?"

She nodded. Prenatal vitamins, extra rest, a strategy to control morning sickness and a plan of action with Abe.

"And you're still not going to tell me what it was?"

She tensed, but shrugged. "Boring, boring."

He shook his head and caught her hand as she reached for her cup of tea. "Nothing about you is boring."

Her heart stuttered at the sensation of his hand around hers. She tried to answer lightly. "You're such a flatterer."

"You know that's not true."

She did, unfortunately. Abe could be brutally honest. It was his greatest strength, but it could hurt sometimes, too. She didn't know how to respond.

"Are you seeing someone else?"

The question sounded as if it had been grudgingly dragged up from the recesses of his stomach. It caught her off guard. "No. Why?"

"You pull back when I touch you. You avoided me this weekend."

"Well, you're leaving soon. I thought it would be better for both of us to back off gradually." Plus there was the matter of her pregnancy, and she couldn't imagine keeping herself on an even keel emotionally if she and Abe continued to be lovers.

"I still want you to come to Washington," he said.

"I'm not."

He pulled back and raked his hand through his hair. "Damn, this is hard. I've always thought you should find someone your own age."

If she were smart, she would let him continue thinking he was too old for her, but the truth was it irritated the hell out of her every time he mentioned their age difference. "That's right. You're ancient and I'm not. Your mind is going, your sight is going. Physically, you've gone to pot. And sexually, you just can't get it up like you used to. Heaven help me if I'd known you when you were younger. I've had a hard enough time keeping up with you as it is."

"You are one mouthy woman," he said, but his eyes were glinting with humor.

Nicola sighed. Lord, the man was just too appealing to her. "Yes, I am. One more reason to kick me to the side of the road," she said and pulled out her PalmPilot and changed the subject. "So what do you have on tap for today? Looks like you're making an appearance with The Christmas Mother Fund Drive and an afternoon meeting with a representative from the Small Business Association. We should leave in—"

She stopped when she felt his hand on hers. She

slowly met his gaze and the intensity in his eyes rendered her mute.

"Nic, I'm serious about wanting you in Washington. I'll do just about anything to make it happen."

Her heart raced at the determination she saw in his face. She knew that when Abe set his mind to something he rarely failed. She would have to draw the line and say no to him. She bit her lip. Six weeks, she told herself. Six weeks. "You can't move Savannah to D.C.," she told him and felt a little hypocritical because her plan was to move to the West Coast once Abe left for Washington.

"I'm putting together an offer. Don't say no right away. I want you to think about it, really think about it. We're a dynamite team."

They were, which added to the pain and shame of it all.

Two

The following day, Abe's phone started ringing.

"Hey, Dad, I got a message that you wanted me to call you about getting together for lunch," his oldest son, Ian, said.

Abe hesitated. He hadn't called Ian for lunch. But hell, he wouldn't turn down the opportunity. He glanced at his calendar. "Right. I have Thursday open. Is that good for you?"

"That will work. Uh, do you have some kind of announcement?"

Abe heard wariness in his son's voice. "Why do you ask that?"

"Well, every time I get a summons, it seems like

there's something big going on. Like you announcing you're running for Senate. Or finding out I have a half sister." He paused. "You haven't had any other children show up, have you?"

"No," Abe said and looked up at the ceiling, shaking his head. "I just wanted to get together with you before I go to Washington."

"For what?" Ian asked.

Abe's gut knotted. Ian's surprise and wariness reminded him yet again of the distance between him and his children. "Because I said so," Abe said.

Silence followed then Ian chuckled. "Okay. That's good enough for me. I'll see you on Thursday."

Just as Abe hung up the phone, there was a tap on his door. "Come in," he called, and Nicola entered the room.

"I just got—" His phone began to ring. "Just a minute. Abe Danforth," he said.

"Hi, it's Adam," another of his sons said. "I hear you want to get together for lunch?"

Abe opened his mouth and hesitated for a half beat, then he looked at Nicola suspiciously. "Yes, I do. You want to do something Saturday or Tuesday?"

"Selene and I have plans on Saturday. How about noon on Tuesday?"

"Good," Abe said and wrote a note to himself.

"Is everything okay?" Adam asked.

"Yes. Why?"

"You haven't asked me to lunch very often. Maybe never. Except when something big is going on."

"No, Adam," Abe said impatiently. "I don't have any other children. I just wanted to get together with you before I go to Washington. Is that good enough?"

Silence followed. "Sure."

"Good. See you on Tuesday," Abe said in a brisk voice and hung up the phone. He locked gazes with Nicola. "What's all this?"

She pushed a lock of hair behind her ear. "Think of it as my little Christmas gift to you."

"What? Opening Pandora's box to the past with two of my sons."

"Well, actually, it won't be just two of them," she said with a hopeful smile.

Abe felt irritation wash over him. "I don't like interference in my private life."

"I guess you could fire me," she suggested in a cheeky voice, ignoring his quiet, serious tone. Abe knew other men had quaked at that tone.

Not Nicola, he thought, exasperated. "This was none of your business."

Hurt flickered across her face, but it was gone before he could focus on it. "I know, but it's been wrenching for me to watch you want to have a better relationship with your children and not do anything about it."

He sighed. "Their resentment is justified."

"To a degree," she said. "On the other hand, you made

sure they were safe, well educated and you encouraged their relationship with your brother, so they would have some stability and support. That's not all bad."

"But I wasn't there," he said, and the blunt fierce truth was unavoidable.

"No you weren't," she said. "And if you could do it over again?"

"I can't," he said firmly. "There's no need to go there." He hated the bitter taste of regret, and in facing each of his children, Abe knew he would be feeling regret with each meeting.

"You don't have to view this as a visit to the guillotine," she said. "You could see it as an opportunity for a new beginning."

"If I lived in Disneyland," he said. "You may be a great campaign manager, but you have no experience being a parent, Nicola," he said. "You have no idea what you've started here."

Her face paled. "Okay, you've made it clear that you're angry that I interfered," she said in a low voice. "We should move on to the business of the day."

The rest of the day their conversation was so stilted and cold he kept thinking he should turn up the heat. He disliked stepping on Nicola's toes, but she shouldn't have nosed into his relationships with his children. Despite the closeness he and Nicola had experienced throughout the campaign, he still had boundaries, and Nicola had violated one in a big way. Every time he thought about facing his grown children's questions, he felt itchy enough to jump out of his skin.

By Thursday when Abe met his son Ian for lunch, Nicola still hadn't thawed. Abe ordered a steak and baked potato. He was in the mood to tear up the meat with his bare teeth.

"How's the coffee business?" Abe asked, focusing his attention on his son.

"Great. It will be even better when the members of the drug cartel that were trying to pressure me are caught." He shook his head. "I'm glad Marc was cleared."

Abe nodded. "And Kate?"

"Is beyond great," Ian said with quiet wonder. He rubbed his jaw. "I didn't see that one coming."

That was how Abe had felt about Nicola. She'd been an unexpected blast of heat from the first moment they'd met. More like an arctic freeze lately.

"Dad?" Ian said. "Dad, is something wrong?"

Abe shook off his distracting thoughts. "No. I just had something on my mind. Back to you and Kate. What are your plans for the holidays?" he asked as the waiter served their meals.

"It required some intense negotiations, but we decided to celebrate Christmas here and join the Fortunes for New Year's Eve."

Abe smiled at his son's wry expression. "Good for you. Kate's got her share of fire, so there will be more negotiations in your future."

Ian cracked a wicked grin. "I look forward to it."

Chuckling, Abe sliced his steak and began to eat. Silence stretched between him and Ian. After he swallowed another bite, Abe glanced up and found his son looking at him with curiosity in his gaze. Abe's stomach sank. *Here come the questions.*

"Did you win your *negotiations* with Mom?" Ian asked.

"There's winning and there's winning," Abe said.

"Sounds like a nonanswer to me," Ian returned.

Abe placed his knife and fork on his plate. He suspected he wouldn't be eating much more. He'd prepared his answer. "Your mother and I wanted different things. She wasn't happy that I was in the military. She wanted me to quit."

Ian leaned back in his chair. "So you had to choose between honor and duty or your wife and family."

Abe narrowed his eyes and sighed. "It was more complicated than that. I had a lot to prove. Especially because of my father. I was a disappointment to him. I didn't perform well in elementary school and I was never a natural student. My father told me he didn't expect me to accomplish much of anything."

Ian's eyes rounded in surprise. "That was harsh."

Abe shrugged. "He was a tough guy. He helped advance the company during a time when more companies were failing than thriving." He paused while his son digested his words. "It was still my choice to pursue my military career. The consequences of that choice are my responsibility and no one else's."

"So why did you have Nicola call to arrange lunch?"

"I wanted some time with my son before I leave for Washington."

Ian nodded his head slowly. "Good enough."

Abe knew he hadn't answered all his son's questions, but he sensed a slight unbending toward him that made his chest feel less tight.

"But what's really on your mind?" Ian asked, taking a bite of his own steak.

Abe stared at his son in consternation. "I just told you—"

Ian waved his hand. "I'm not talking about you and me and lunch. I'm talking about what had you distracted a few minutes ago."

Abe approved his son's keen observational skills. No wonder Ian was so successful. He rubbed his lip, considering whether he should discuss his concerns with his son. A strange prospect, he thought, but his son had grown into a strong man, a trustworthy man. He felt a surge of pride. "I want Nicola to come to Washington with me. She insists she's not interested. I'm stumped."

Ian took a swallow of coffee. "Do you want her on staff?"

Confused, Abe wrinkled his forehead. "Of course. How else?"

Silence followed and Ian cleared his throat. "I didn't know if you had a more personal interest in her."

"She's too young," Abe immediately said.

Ian nodded, but said nothing.

"She should find someone her own age."

Ian remained silent.

"It would be incredibly foolish for a man my age with my less-than-stellar history with romantic relationships to get seriously involved with a woman almost twenty years younger than I am."

Ian glanced away then met his gaze dead-on. "But do you want her?"

His son's direct question hit him like a lead pipe. He took a moment to catch his breath.

Ian shrugged. "It's none of my business, but it seems to me that if you meet a woman who makes your world turn, then you shouldn't pass up the chance of keeping her in your world. No disrespect intended, but you're not getting any younger. If you want Nicola like I wanted Kate, then you'd better go after her full throttle. Or you'll regret it the rest of your life."

Abe looked at his son, torn between surprise at his son's directness and amusement at his predicament. "When did you turn into such a blunt, bottom-line man?"

Ian met his gaze and a whisper of a grin lifted his lips. "It's hereditary."

Summoned to his highness's inner sanctum with a crisp, perfunctory request via Crofthaven's paging system, Nicola walked toward his office. She knew Abe had met Ian for lunch today and probably still had his nose out of joint over her calling his children on his behalf without his knowledge. Fine, she told herself. She hated it when Abe was displeased with her, but maybe in some crazy way, his anger would make it easier for them to part. Her heart twisted at the thought. Sometimes it was still hard for her to believe she was pregnant. Until the intermittent nausea or need for a nap hit her. When she thought about raising a child by herself, she fought the surge of panic and told herself she could do it. She would do it.

Mentally girding herself, she lifted her hand to knock on his office door just as it was whipped open. Abe closed the space between them, took her hand and tugged her inside the office, pushing the door closed behind her. He lowered his mouth to hers for a lingering kiss and pulled back. "Thanks for interfering."

Her heart racing, she blinked at him in surprise. "What?"

He lifted his lips in a heart-stopping smile and the sensual glint in his eyes produced the effect of melting her. "Thanks for interfering. I had lunch with Ian today. It was good."

Nicola felt her chest expand in relief. She hadn't realized she'd been so tense. "I'm glad." What an understatement. She was thrilled and wanted to know more. "What did you talk about? Did he ask sticky questions?"

"We talked about several things, and yes, he did ask some sticky questions, but it went well." He paused and chuckled. "I was surprised at how much like me he can be. Never would have thought it."

She heard the pride in his voice and smiled. "Chip off the old block?"

"I wouldn't go that far," he said. "I'm glad Ian didn't have my learning difficulties. One thing I made damn certain was that the kids got tutors if they needed them."

Nicola felt a lump in her throat. "You told Ian about your learning disability?" she asked, surprised.

Abe lifted his hand and shook his head. "Not specifically. I told him I wasn't a good student."

"Close enough for now," she said and felt her heart squeeze tight. If she couldn't share Abe's life, then she wanted him to have a better relationship with his children. "I've wanted this for you for a long time."

He met her gaze. "I've wanted you for a long time," he said in a low, rough voice.

Nicola's heart stopped in her chest. Her throat turned dry. "We agreed that we should keep our relationship professional. You'll be leaving."

Abe shook his head and closed the space between them. "You agreed. I didn't. And if I have anything to say about it, you'll be going to Washington with me."

* * *

Two days later, Nicola felt as if she were playing dodgeball with Abe. For every step she took away from him, it seemed he took two toward her. He'd invited her to dinner three nights in a row. She'd successfully avoided him the first two, but since she had accompanied him to an appearance that ran late, she had no valid excuse tonight.

Despite the fact that the trendy, romantic restaurant was packed, Abe tipped the host an extra twenty and she and he were seated at a lovely corner table with a view of the water.

"What can I get you to drink?" the waiter asked.

"Wine?" Abe asked.

Nicola shook her head. No more drinking for her. Alcohol wasn't good for growing babies. "Water. I'm very thirsty tonight."

A few minutes later, the waiter took their food orders. Nicola went with grilled chicken and vegetables. No seafood until she could remember which fish had too much mercury. She'd skimmed an article, but couldn't remember the exact details.

"I'm surprised you didn't get the tuna. Isn't it one of your favorites?" Abe asked.

He'd noticed. The knowledge sent a tiny forbidden thrill. She shrugged. The prospect of eating tuna made her stomach turn. "I'm in the mood for something different."

Abe nodded and reached for her hand, surprising the

stuffing out of her. He'd always been careful to avoid public displays of affection. "What are you doing?" she asked and tried to pull her hand back.

"I'm holding your hand. What's the problem?" he asked, still holding her hand in his.

She glanced around. "What if people are looking?"

"Then they'll know the truth," he said in a voice so calm it made her nuts. "We have a personal relationship."

"No, we don't," she whispered, then corrected herself when she saw Abe's lifted eyebrow. "Yes, we do, but we don't need to share it with the world."

"Don't you think you're overreacting? I'm just holding your hand, not going at it with you in the coat closet, although…" His voice trailed off, suggesting he wouldn't mind doing all kinds of things with her in the coat closet.

Feeling heat rise to her cheeks, Nicola grabbed her glass of water and took a gulp. Spying the waiter heading toward them with bread and salads, she jerked her hand away from his. "Behave," she told him in as stern a voice as she could manage.

After the waiter served the salads, Nicola took a deep breath to calm herself and picked up her fork to take a bite of salad. She felt Abe's hand on her leg just above her knee and her fork fell from her hand, clattering to her plate.

Staring at him in amazement, she put her hand over his to remove it. "What is with you?"

He turned his hand over and laced his fingers through hers, and the tender gesture disconcerted her.

"I miss you," he said, holding her gaze.

Her heart stopped and she could hardly bear to look at him. She would have to leave him. She couldn't continue leading him or herself on. She bit her lip. "How can you miss me? I haven't gone anywhere."

"Yes, you have. I know you have feelings for me. Why are you avoiding me?"

Because I don't deserve you. Because I'm pregnant. Because if the truth came out, it could hurt you and I never ever want to do that. "I told you that since you're leaving, I thought it would be easier on both of us if we backed away from so much—" *Wonderful sex. Spending so much time with you that it makes me only want to be with you more.* She broke off and cleared her throat "—personal interaction," she finally said.

"I disagree," he said in a gentle voice that possessed an underlying firmness that she'd learned meant he wasn't budging. "I think we should make the most of the time we have left. Especially if you're not coming to D.C. But for the record, Nicola, I will do my best to change your mind."

Nicola saw the rock-hard determination in Abe's eyes and knew she was in big trouble.

Three

In the limousine, Nicola's cell phone rang as she went over notes for the speech Abe would give to the businessmen's association in approximately twenty minutes. "Sorry. Excuse me just a moment," she said to Abe and pulled her phone from her purse.

"Miss Granville. Carolyn Hopkins returning your call about the furnished town house on King Street. It's still available, and I'll rent it month to month with a substantial deposit."

"Oh, that's fabulous. How soon can I move in?"

"It's ready now. Already been cleaned."

"I'll take it," Nicola said.

"Move," Abe echoed, his voice oozing surprise and displeasure. "When did you decide to—"

Nicola bit her lip. She hadn't exactly figured out how to tell Abe she was moving out, but she'd decided moving was necessary. It was too difficult trying to keep the secret of her pregnancy from him twenty-four hours a day. It was too difficult resisting him twenty-four hours a day. She'd been hoping for something nonconfrontational and cowardly like an e-mail. "Thanks so much. I'll stop by tomorrow with the deposit. Bye for now." She disconnected and turned back to the speech. "I think this group will be especially interested in your stand on tax breaks for small business and—"

"Why in hell are you moving?" Abe interrupted. "And when were you planning to tell me? After you'd left? Via e-mail?"

Nicola winced. Sometimes it was very inconvenient the way Abe could see straight through her. "I'm moving because it's not necessary for me to be at Crofthaven any longer. If you recall, the reason I originally moved to Crofthaven was because we were working sixteen hours a day and I was tempted to sleep in my car instead of driving home." She saw him open his mouth and surged onward. "Things are different now. We're not moving at a frantic pace anymore."

"I thought you liked Crofthaven."

Her heart twisted. How could she not love a home so steeped in family history when her longest stay at a foster home was eighteen months as a teenager? "I do. The history and elegance of it, and it's beautiful for the holidays."

"So what's the rush to leave?" he asked, studying her.

Nicola resisted the urge to squirm. "I just don't think it's appropriate for me to stay at Crofthaven now that the election is over. I don't think it looks right."

He shook off her explanation. "Crofthaven is huge. And it's not as if you're staying in my bedroom or I'm staying in yours," he said, his eyes glinting with heat and the barest hint of challenge.

She felt a rush of warmth at the flood of images that raced through her mind. True, she thought. She and Abe hadn't spent a lot of time in her bed or his. Their love-making had been more spontaneous. More than once, they had sexually combusted in his office, and there'd been that time in the limo. Her mouth went dry at the sensual memory. She picked up her bottle of water and took a long, cool swallow.

The limo thankfully pulled to a stop in front of the hotel hosting the businessmen's association meeting. "Oh, look at that. We're here already." She scrambled to gather her material.

Abe covered her hand with his. "Nic, what's going on? You're not acting like yourself."

Her heart hammered in her chest and she reminded herself that despite the fact that Abe seemed to be able to read her like a book, he did not have an internal sonogram and could not know she was pregnant unless she told him. "It's just a different stage in the project. The campaign has wound down and you're gearing up for your move to Washington. I'm taking some time to assess my options." There, she thought, that sounded calm and businesslike.

Abe looked at her for a long moment, then chuckled and shook his head. "Bull." He lifted her hand to his mouth. "You're running. I wonder why."

Her breath hitched in her throat. *You don't want to know. Trust me, you don't want to know.* "The only running we're doing right now is running late," she said, pulling her hand from his and tapping her watch. "We need to get inside for the meeting."

Nicola scooted inside the hotel to make sure everything was in order for Abe's arrival then returned with a representative from the businessmen's association to greet Abe and accompany him to the ballroom where he would speak.

As soon as Abe walked through the doorway, the speaker at the podium stopped. "Ladies and gentlemen, there's our new senator. Abraham Danforth."

The crowd erupted in applause, rising to their feet. Nicola felt a swell of pride for Abe's popularity. He'd worked hard and he'd earned the respect of the people.

"This could go to my head," Abe murmured to her as he smiled and waved. "If I didn't have you around to keep me on the ground."

Nicola's heart twisted. "You don't need the ground, Abe. You're flying."

For a sliver of an instant, he looked as if he was going to argue, but then he seemed to remember he was on the job. "Later," he said, promising a sticky discussion with that one word.

Nicola would do her best to make sure later was never.

Even though she knew it was for the best, Nicola didn't enjoy packing her things the next morning. She'd been too exhausted the previous evening to do more than fall into bed. Dressed in a terry robe with her hair still wet from her shower, she transferred as many of her sweaters and slacks as she could from the cherry dresser to her suitcase.

Packing reminded her of her teen years, which had felt like one move after another. The social worker had assured her that the moves weren't her fault. Her foster families had loved her, but circumstances had always pushed her out. A divorce, job loss, a move. Even today Nicola knew rationally that her foster families' decisions not to keep her weren't because they hadn't cared for her, but it didn't stop the knot in her stomach. She'd always feared not being wanted.

This time was different, she told herself. Abe wanted her to stay.

But if he knew the truth, he wouldn't.

Her stomach knotted again. She tried to ignore it, but

her anxiety wasn't helping her already tenuous stomach. Sinking into an overstuffed chair, she took a tiny bite of a cracker and sipped her decaf tea.

She glanced around the beautifully appointed room and remembered other small rooms where she'd slept. Wriggling her bare toes into the plush carpet, she sighed at the combination of indulgence and class. Gleaming cherry dresser and armoire, a cherry desk and hutch that housed her computer, fax and printer, were counterbalanced by the chaise lounge upholstered in yellow-and-rose cotton sateen, draperies in coordinating fabric that permitted privacy or when pulled back allowed the sun to stream in from the floor-to-ceiling windows. Top it all off with a king-size bed with a mattress that even Goldilocks would have agreed was *just right* and who wouldn't be in heaven?

Nicola gave a wry, silent chuckle to herself. Crofthaven was a different world for a girl from the wrong side of the tracks in rural Georgia. The luxury of the place was almost sinful. The staff answered her every need. Sheesh, she remembered the time she'd offended the housekeeper by fixing her own breakfast.

A woman could grow accustomed to being spoiled like that. If that woman weren't Nicola. Nicola had never forgotten this was temporary.

Like so many things in her life had been. Temporary father, temporary mother, temporary families. She'd continued the theme with her career, moving from one public relations assignment to the next. For her, the allure of Crofthaven wasn't the luxury. It was the heritage that seeped through the walls. Generations of Danforths had laughed and cried here. When she inhaled, she felt as if she were breathing in the essence of family. Despite the fact that Abe felt as if he'd failed as a father, he'd provided a place and a sense of tradition for his children. They knew who they were. They knew what being a Danforth meant and no matter where they were, they knew they weren't really alone.

Nicola had been alone for a long time. She slid her hand over her belly protectively. Not anymore. She had another little someone in her life and she would do her best to be everything her baby needed.

A knock interrupted her thoughts. It was probably the housekeeper. "Come in."

Abe walked into her room and she stood, caught off guard. Her heart leaped. Tall, confident, strong and smart, he was everything she'd wanted in a man without knowing it.

His gaze fell over her and she immediately felt underdressed. Abe was the kind of man who required her to be on her toes and at her best all the time. She saw him look at her suitcase and her stomach sank. *Uh-oh.*

"It's silly for you to move," he said. "If you come with me to Washington—"

"Which I'm not," she reminded him.

He clenched his jaw. "Even if you don't, then there's

still no need for you to move out right now." He paused. "Do you hate Crofthaven so much?"

"Not at all," she said, surprised at his suggestion. "What's not to love? It's beautiful."

He shrugged. "It can seem cold sometimes. The kids probably hated the formality of it. My brother and I did sometimes."

"I think Crofthaven is fabulous," she assured him. "It's more than the furnishings or the building. It's that your family has lived here for generations."

"You mention that a lot," he said. "But you never say much about your own family."

She waved her hand. "Oh, they were very different from the Danforths."

"Different doesn't have to mean worse."

"In this case it does," she said, but kept her tone light.

"I remember you saying you didn't have any brothers or sisters."

"That's right."

"And your mother?"

"She passed away a long time ago. I was ten."

He cocked his head to one side. "Did you live with your father?"

"No," she said, feeling incredibly uncomfortable. The main thing she remembered about her father was that he'd abandoned her and her mother long before her mother got sick. "Could we please stop? I don't like talking about this."

Abe paused and she could tell he had many more questions and wanted answers to all of them. "I wouldn't judge you," he finally said in a quiet voice. "My failures and lack of judgment have been paraded in front of you and everyone. It occurs to me that you know everything about me and I don't know half as much about you." His gaze held hers and she felt a slow tug in her belly. It was the same sensation she felt falling down a long, steep hill. A hill named Abraham Danforth.

"You know enough," she said.

He shook his head. "You've fascinated me. You've been a strong, vibrant, sexy, caring woman throughout the campaign. But there's more to you than that. I haven't seen the soft underbelly."

"I prefer to keep my underbelly protected," she said, feeling tense at the determined, intuitive expression in his eyes. Being Abe's campaign manager and lover had been exhilarating. The prospect of having his undivided attention for more than a night, however, terrified Nicola. Both of them had been so focused on the campaign that their lovemaking had felt like an overflow of the energy they generated together. His attitude suggested something more, something deeper.

"I can protect your underbelly or anything else that needs protecting," he said in a husky voice that made her blood feel like warm honey sliding through her veins.

She forced a smile. "Thanks, but no thanks. I don't need a protector. I'm a big girl."

"I'll say," he said, his gaze sliding over her curves in masculine appreciation. He stepped closer and she felt the sexual click between them. "But there's need and there's want. A big girl doesn't have to just settle for what she needs. She can get what she wants." He lowered his head and pressed his mouth against hers, tempting more than taking. Her body responded with breathtaking speed.

He slid his tongue over her lips, and he tasted like the most delicious, decadent candy she'd ever eaten.

And she was supposed to be on a strict diet, a diet which did not include tasting Abe. Nicola tried to pry her lips from his. She really did, but her mouth wasn't listening to her brain. He just felt so good.

Abe did the pulling back. "What do you want, Nic?"

Her heart pounding a mile a minute, she inhaled and instantly regretted it. She loved the way his aftershave smelled on him. He didn't wear too much, just enough to make her want to bury her face in his throat. She shook her head and stepped back. "Sometimes what we want isn't the best thing for us," she said, wishing her voice didn't sound so breathless. "You are like Godiva chocolates. Eating too many of those will make me fat."

"Ah, but you forget. I'm calorie free. You won't gain any weight from indulging in me."

Nicola swallowed a hysterical laugh and coughed. *Calorie free?* The man had no idea, no clue. She would be the size of a beached whale before this was all over.

* * *

Abe sat across from his son Adam and stirred his coffee. Despite his best efforts to dissuade her, Nicola had moved out and Abe had spent the entire weekend without her and not liking it.

Adam took a sip of his coffee, running an assessing glance around the original D&D coffee shop for which he was a partner. "Good to see they're keeping up with the Christmas rush. We have a Christmas blend we've put together and it's moving so fast we can barely keep it in stock." He glanced at his father. "Guess everyone needs an extra jolt of java during the holidays. How do you like it?"

"Not bad," Abe said. "Cinnamon?"

"Right you are."

"Not all my taste buds have died yet," Abe said, cracking a grin.

Adam's forehead wrinkled. "What do you mean dying taste buds? Do you have a health problem?"

"Yes. It's called getting older. Taste buds die as you age. One more thing that goes—like hearing, your knees, your hair."

"Hmm," Adam said thoughtfully and paused for a moment. "Does this have anything to do with Nicola?"

Abe frowned. "Why do you ask?"

Adam shrugged. "Just Ian mentioned that you might be interested in her as more than a campaign manager. No big deal."

"What do you mean no big deal? She's almost twenty years younger than I am."

"Yeah, but you take care of yourself. You seem younger. Besides, maybe she's not interested in young guys."

"I don't know why not," Abe said, taking another sip of his holiday java.

"Are you trying to convince me or yourself?" Adam asked, impatience cutting into his tone. "If the purpose for this meeting was to get my blessing for you to have a personal relationship with Nicola, you've got it."

Abe was speechless. "The purpose of this meeting was to spend some one-on-one time with you before I move to D.C. Why in hell do you think this is about Nicola?"

"Ian said you seemed pretty tripped up about her. He told me the stuff about how you and Mom weren't all that happy, too."

Abe sighed. "Has this been discussed among all of my children?"

"Well, yeah," Adam said. "It's not like any of us have had the most open relationship in the world with you. If any of us gets a peek into your secret window, we share."

"Am I still that unapproachable?"

"Yes and no," Adam said. "You've set the bar pretty high for all of us, and none of us want to be the one to pull down the Danforth image. I was surprised to hear that you ever had academic problems. It was reassuring to hear you weren't completely perfect."

"That's what Nicola said when she found out about it," he said, remembering the late, late night when his brain couldn't sort out the words in front of him. "Dyslexia. She found out by accident about 3:00 a.m. when I kept twisting words I was reading for a speech. I was too tired to read straight."

Adam dropped his jaw. "You're dyslexic?"

"Yes," Abe said, feeling a strange combination of vulnerability and relief. "That was why I made sure all of you had access to tutors if you needed them."

"I'm surprised Uncle Harold didn't ever mention it." He took a sip of his coffee. "Maybe he was trying to keep the myth alive."

Abe nodded. His brother was one of the great gifts of his life. "Maybe. That sounds like him, doesn't it?"

"Yeah. So Nicola got it out of you. That woman is sharp as a whip. A man would be stupid to let her get away. No way I was going to let Selene get away. I had to be creative and crafty as hell, but she was worth the trouble."

Curious, Abe met Adam's gaze. "Creative and crafty in what way?"

"I couldn't let her know exactly who I was at first. I sent her gifts. I used the message board in the shop to lure her," he said, cocking his head toward the board where customers posted messages. "I understand more than one romance has gotten started there."

Abe shook his head at his son's tactics. Abe had always been more direct. His relationships with women during the last few years had felt more like business arrangements than passionate affairs. With the exception of Nicola.

"Enough about me," Abe muttered. "How's everything with the wedding? Is Selene okay?"

"The wedding is December 12 at 7:00 p.m. Just in case you forgot to pencil it in your calendar."

Abe recognized the cynicism in his son's voice. Adam thought Abe had never paid any attention to him, but he was wrong. "I knew that. How are Selene and her father?" he asked knowing that Selene had felt terribly betrayed by her father for trying to use her to save his political career.

Adam's gaze softened. "A little better," he said. "Nice of you to ask," he added grudgingly.

"It's become tradition that the groom's parents fund the honeymoon, but I'm sure you and Selene already have plans."

"Sure do."

Abe pulled a deed and map from his breast pocket. "So I bought you an island instead."

Adam gaped at him. "Excuse me?"

"I bought you an island in the Caribbean. Very small. There are some legends that pirates frequented it. I thought since you're a history buff, you might like that."

Adam unfolded the deed and map and shook his head. "You're kidding, aren't you?"

"No," Abe said. "It doesn't make up for the fact that I've been so unavailable all these years, but it's a personal token from me to you. I'm proud of you."

Adam stared at the papers then glanced at Abe. "Was this Nicola's idea?"

Abe felt a pinch of regret. In the past it would have been too close to the truth. "No. She suggested the honeymoon, and another option was a check. I wanted to give you something more personal."

"I don't know what to say."

"You don't need to say anything," Abe said. He knew he couldn't buy back the years he'd been gone or distracted with the challenge of the moment. "I'm sorry I wasn't around for you much when you were growing up. You're a grown man, successful. You don't need me now, but if you ever do need something, I'd be honored if you give me a call."

Adam glanced down and drummed his thumbs on the table. He lifted his head and looked at Abe skeptically. "This is a switch for you. What brought it on?"

Abe's chest tightened at how many twists and turns his life had taken during the last year. "I've spent a lot of time running. I always thought I was running up my next mountain, but I think I may have been running away from my failures as much as anything. It may seem like I spent the last year talking, but I found out quickly that I had to do more listening. You can't fix something you won't face."

"It's pretty late for that," Adam said.

Abe's chest tightened further. "Yeah, but I couldn't face myself if I didn't try."

Adam sat quietly for a long moment. "So maybe the old dog can learn a new trick or two after all," he said. "Time will tell."

"It will," Abe said. He'd known Adam wouldn't change his mind after one cup of coffee and a wedding gift. "Thanks for working me into your schedule," he said, grinning at his son.

"Maybe we can do it again sometime," Adam said.

"I'd like that," Abe said.

"Okay, just one more thing." Adam rubbed his chin and chuckled. "Nicola. You need to pick a position."

Taken aback by the abrupt change in subject, Abe lifted his eyebrows. "What do you mean?"

"It's just like your campaign. You need to choose where you stand on the issue of Nicola. If you figure out you want her, then you need to fight like hell to get her."

Four

Abe had originally planned to reduce his personal appearances during December to allow both him and Nicola to recover from the frantic pace of the campaign. He had envisioned sharing quiet dinners and private evenings with her. Now that she'd moved out of Crofthaven and found an excuse to refuse all his social invitations, he was forced to take another approach if he wanted time with Nicola.

"I've been asked to attend a holiday party at the governor's mansion. Since the press will be there, I'd like you to go with me," he said as she joined him for tea and toast on Thursday morning. He wondered when she'd switched coffee to tea. "You're not on a diet, are you? Your body is perfect."

She blinked at him. "I'm not on a diet, although I could usually stand to lose a few pounds." She cleared her throat. "Thank you for the compliment," she said in a low voice.

"You don't need to lose an ounce," he said, running his gaze over her voluptuous frame, remembering how she'd felt naked in his arms, rubbing against him. He felt himself grow warm at the image. "Your body is great the way it is." *I could show you just how great your body is,* he thought.

She bit her lip and looked away. "Thanks." She cleared her throat and sipped her tea. "When is the governor's Christmas Ball?"

"Saturday night."

She made a choking sound. "*This* Saturday night?"

He nodded. "It's formal with a sit-down dinner. It will probably run late. We can stay overnight in Atlanta."

"Oh, that won't be necessary," she said.

He heard a rare trace of nervousness in her voice. He didn't know whether to be irritated or encouraged. "I don't want to get back at two in the morning if I don't have to. We had to do enough of that during the campaign."

She met his gaze and he saw an argument brewing in her eyes. "Okay. Separate rooms."

"Of course," he said. *Separate, but adjoining.*

"And there's Adam and Selene's wedding in a few days," he continued down his list.

"That's a family event, so I didn't expect to attend," she said.

"You don't want to be there for Adam's wedding?" Abe asked.

She opened her mouth and looked away. "Of course I do. I just didn't want to impose."

"You're not imposing. My children see you as family, maybe more than they do me," he added dryly.

"How did it go with Adam?" she asked in that soft, sensitive voice that made him think she cared more than she thought she should.

"He's justifiably cynical, but I think he might be open to having coffee with me again."

She sighed and shook her head. "I know you weren't there for them the way they wanted you to be, but you did provide for them and made sure they were safe, well educated and supported by your brother." She stood. "The lack of perspective makes me a little crazy sometimes."

"What perspective should they have?"

She made a sound of frustration. "Well, for one thing, they didn't have to move around a lot. They always had a place they could call home. They didn't have to worry they'd have to make a midnight move and end up with a totally different set of guardians. Trust me. Things could have been much, much worse for them."

Abe had heard Nicola mention the same opinion before, but he'd felt too guilty to allow anything she said to penetrate his sense of failure. He looked at her standing next to the window with her arms crossed over her chest and something inside him clicked. He walked toward her. "Is that how it was for you?"

Color rose to her cheeks and she shook her head. "I'm sorry. I probably shouldn't have vented like that. This is your business, not mine."

He chuckled. "It's never stopped you before. Why should it stop you now?" He wanted to touch her, but instead stuck his hands in his pockets. "You didn't answer my question. Was that how it was for you?"

She glanced away. "I don't really like talking about it—"

"Please," he said and watched her eyes widen in surprise.

Clearly conflicted, she closed her eyes for a moment, then opened them. "When my mother died, there was no one to take care of me. I grew up in foster homes. Several of them. They were mostly nice people who just had bad luck. One of them lost a job. One couple got a divorce. So when I hear your kids being cold to you after you gave them so much more than I could have dreamed of having, it makes me angry."

Abe was surprised and felt foolish for not having learned about Nicola's childhood before, but she'd always evaded the subject. "You've come a long way, baby."

Her mouth lifted in a wistful smile. "That I have."

"Why didn't you ever get married?" he couldn't help asking.

"I've always had a busy, satisfying career and I never found the right guy," she said with a shrug.

His gut twisted at the admission. He would have to think about that later. "But you would marry if you found the right guy?"

She glanced out the window. "Not everyone finds the right person and even if they do, sometimes things still don't work out."

"That doesn't sound like you."

She looked at him. "What do you mean?"

"I mean, during the campaign you were always saying nothing is impossible until you've tried everything."

"That was the campaign," she said with a smile. "Not my personal life."

"But you've said the same thing about my relationship with my children, too."

She began to fiddle with her fingers. Nicola never fidgeted, Abe thought.

"Then maybe it's romance. Romance is so emotional you can't really control it. It's hard to choose who you fall for, if they fall for you and if it's a good time in your life or his life to get together. That kind of thing." She laughed. "I don't really have time to be looking for my dream man right now. Too many other things to do."

Nicola felt as if she'd been run over by a truck. "And the truck's name is Abraham Danforth," she muttered to herself as she stumbled from the bathroom to the couch for the third time in an hour. She was glad she'd had the foresight to negotiate getting today off. Abe had argued against it, but she'd stood her ground, pointing out that she'd be working Saturday night at the Governor's Christmas Ball. With her morning sickness kicking in big-time, all she wanted to do was lie on the sofa dressed in her old sweats while she moaned and indulged in a pity party.

She closed her eyes against the unsteady feeling in her tummy. "It will pass," she told herself. "It will pass." Nicola wished she could forget hearing a woman in the doctor's office comment on how her morning sickness had lasted nine months.

She slid her hand over her tummy. Despite the nausea, she felt protective of the little life growing inside her. *Sugar Cookie,* she called the baby and smiled. She just hoped that she could learn to be a good mother. Her number one fear was that she had no normal maternal instincts. How could she when she had given her first baby up for adoption so many years ago?

But she would learn, she told herself. She would read books and take classes. When she wasn't hyperventilating from anxiety or dodging her feelings for Abe, she even felt a little excited. She wondered if the baby was a boy or girl. She had no doubt that Sugar Cookie would have the trademark Danforth determination.

An image of Abe slid through her mind and her heart

picked up. He was acting different lately, more focused on her, more inquisitive. He knew her body and as much of her mind as she had allowed, but now he seemed determined to learn the rest of her.

She covered her eyes with her hand and tried to stop thinking about him. Even a twelve-step program wouldn't help her get Abe out of her system at this point because she was forced to see the man nearly every day. Thank goodness she was Abe-free today and she could shore up her defenses.

After a short nap, she ate chicken noodle soup and soda crackers then started a load of laundry. The town house was nice, a little too quiet, but that was what she needed. She didn't need the tradition and sense of family at Crofthaven. She needed to get her head screwed on straight without Abe's influence.

Folding a towel, she heard a ringing sound and it took a full moment for her to realize it was her doorbell. "Who is this? No one knows I'm here yet," she muttered as she made her way down the steps. She looked through the peephole and her stomach dipped. Glancing down at her sweat suit, she swore under her breath.

The doorbell rang again.

She reluctantly opened the door to Abe holding a Christmas tree and two large bags. "Merry Christmas, Nic. I didn't want you to miss having a tree because of your move."

Nicola's heart tightened in her chest. Christmas had often been an iffy holiday when she was a child. After a few years of being shuffled around, she'd conditioned herself not to expect much. Even now, she gave donations, but downplayed her private celebration. The tree was a surprise and a reminder that she would be celebrating the holidays with her baby next year.

"Thank you," she said to Abe, unable to keep a smile from her face. "This is a terrific surprise and I probably wouldn't have thought of getting one until none were left."

"I picked up some ornaments and lights, too. Just in case yours are packed away somewhere inconvenient."

"Looks like you thought of everything," she said, taking the bags and peeking inside.

"Hope so. I'll help you put it up this afternoon," he said as he carried the tree inside the town house.

Nicola opened her mouth to refuse then paused as dismay shot through her. What an ungrateful witch she'd be if she said, "*Thanks for the tree, you can leave now.*" She sighed. "You don't have to do that. I know you're busy."

"Not that busy," he said. "What about you? Do you have plans this evening?"

She considered saying yes, but knew her sweat suit would negate her words. "Not really. I just planned to relax. I've been a bum most of the day."

He studied her for a long moment and lifted his

hand to her cheek. "Are you not feeling well, again? You look pale."

Oh, don't go there, she thought and shook off his concern. "I didn't bother with blush today. It's not very chivalrous of you to comment on my lack of makeup," she chided him, trying to keep it light.

"Then I'll try to make up for it by getting Chinese dinner delivered tonight while we put up the tree."

Panic stabbed at her. This afternoon was turning into tonight. And Chinese food? Her stomach protested at the very thought. "Not necessary," she said. "I just had some soup a little while ago."

"Okay, then let's get started on the tree," he said.

She smothered a laugh, but he must have caught her.

"What's funny?"

"Your military background comes out sometimes. For instance, just now I felt as if I was supposed to snap my heels together, salute and say, 'Yessir!'" She lifted her hand in a mock salute.

His eyes glinted with dark humor and he moved closer to her. "That's not all bad, you mouthy private. Now if I could just get that reaction from you on everything."

Her heart bumped. "You wouldn't like me if I was a yes-man."

"Maybe not, but I'm game for a trial. You say yes to everything I ask."

"In your dreams, Senator," she scoffed.

His face turned serious and he lifted his hand to her

cheek. "You've been there more than you know, Nic. You've been in my dreams."

Her breath hitched in her throat. "That's me," she tried to joke, but her voice came out a little husky. "Nightmare Nicola."

He chuckled and kissed her quickly before she could back away. "No nightmares, Nic. I promise." He let his hand fall to his side. "But I also promised to help put up your tree and that's what I'm going to do."

He had the tree up in the stand in no time and the smell of fresh pine helped drag Nicola into more of a holiday mood. She put on some apple cider and found a radio station playing Christmas music.

She helped Abe with the lights then they started with the ornaments. He pulled open one of the bags. "I didn't know what kind of ornaments you would like. The clerk said the fashion trend for trees this season is sophisticated white and red." He pulled out boxes of red-and-white ornaments. "Then she said there are always people who love the Victorian angels. Some do their entire tree in them. I didn't think you were the Victorian type, but I thought you wouldn't mind a few angels." He pulled out three angels. "And the rest are some I liked."

Touched and curious, she was drawn to the ornaments Abe had said he liked. "Sourdough!" she said, touching three ornaments of winter-clothes clad children with tiny candy canes all made out of sourdough. "I love them. And look at the rest. A Christmas clown,

Christmas shells, a Christmas sailor." She looked at him in surprise. "Abe, these are fabulous. How long did you spend looking?"

He shrugged. "Not that long. My rule was if I liked it or thought you might like it then I bought it."

Her heart felt mushy and she felt her eyes burn. *Oh, no, not tears.* She batted her eyelids quickly to keep from crying.

"What's wrong?"

"Nothing. I think I've got something in my eye. This was so wonderful of you. I don't know what to say. No one has ever brought me a Christmas tree with all the trimmings." She swallowed hard over the lump of emotion in her throat.

"You're crying," Abe said in amazement. "I've never seen you cry. Come here." He reached for her.

"No, no, no," she said, but he ignored her protests and sat down in a chair and pulled her onto his lap. If he touched her, that would only make it harder for her to pull herself together. She closed her eyes and felt a tear slide down her cheek.

Abe held her against him as if she was a child. "What made you cry?"

She took a shallow breath. "It was just so nice. I'm not used to it."

"Not used to someone being nice to you?" His voice had a rough growl. "You've been hanging around the wrong people."

Nicola sighed and smiled. "Well thanks for the tree and everything and forgive me for my weepy moment."

Abe slid his hand to her chin and turned her head to meet his gaze. "My pleasure to be here for both."

He was going to kill her, she thought as her heart constricted again. She tried to rise, but he held her close.

"Not so fast," he said.

"We still need to decorate the tree," she said, knowing it wasn't a good idea for her to sit on Abe's lap for more than three seconds. There was still too much chemistry between them.

"That can wait. I want you to do something for me. Close your eyes. I'm not taking your sweatshirt off," he assured her. "I want to, but I'm not. Just close your eyes."

With her heart still hammering in her chest, she closed her eyes.

"Pretend you're ten. What did you want for Christmas?"

She saw herself at that age, so forlorn yet hopeful. "I asked Santa to make my mother well."

"Oh, sweetie." Abe swore and smoothed her hair.

"That was something my mother always did," she murmured, remembering the gentle way her mother had handled her hair. "She played with my hair. It was the most soothing thing in the world. Hmm," she said with a soft laugh and opened her eyes. "I hadn't thought about that in forever."

Abe put his hand over her eyes. "We're not finished."

She made a sound of frustration. "Okay, but if I do it, then you have to, too."

Abe paused. "Okay," he grumbled. "You're fifteen years old. What do you want for Christmas?"

"To live in the same house for the rest of my life," she said without thinking. "An album by Jon Bon Jovi and a pair of jeans that aren't hand-me-downs, all the books Louisa May Alcott wrote and a sister or brother." Remembering her childhood made her feel vulnerable as hell. She lifted Abe's hand from her eyes. "Okay, enough about me. Your turn. Close your eyes."

"I haven't thought about this in a long time," he protested.

"Too bad. Neither had I. Close your eyes," she said and covered his eyes when he didn't immediately close them. "Okay, you're eight years old. What do you want for Christmas?"

"I want to read a one-hundred-page book. I want to get grades that won't make my father disappointed in me. I want a G.I. Joe and a tank."

Nicola smiled at the bittersweet combination of his wishes. "You must have been a Navy SEAL in the womb."

He chuckled. "My boot camp instructor would disagree."

"Okay, you're sixteen, what do you want for Christmas?"

"That's easy. A car or the use of a vehicle so I can

take my girlfriend out and we can make out in the back seat and if I get lucky, maybe…"

"Did you?" Nicola asked, curious.

"Not that year," he said with a rakish grin.

"Probably a good thing. Potent Pete," she muttered and moved to stand.

He pulled back. "Hey. Where'd that come from?"

"Nothing," she said. "I was just thinking that you seem to impregnate without problems. If you'd started too young, you might have even more children."

He shrugged. "Maybe so. Thank goodness I'm done with that now. I hear one of the advantages of getting older is that a man's swimmers aren't as good as they used to be."

I wouldn't count on that. She bit her tongue to keep from saying it aloud.

Five

Dressed in green satin with her red hair floating over her creamy shoulders, Nicola looked like a combination of exquisite jewels, emerald for her dress and eyes, ruby for her lips and pearl for her skin.

Abe took her hand. "You take my breath away."

She smiled. "I find that difficult to believe, Senator. You're as rock steady as they come."

He called her bluff and lifted her hand to his chest. "Then how do you explain that?" he asked, knowing his heart was pounding.

She glanced down and her eyelids shielded her expression from him. "Sugar rush? Caffeine high?"

He groaned. "Or maybe it's you. You look beautiful, Nicola."

She met his gaze impishly. "So do you."

He blinked. "I can honestly say I've never been called beautiful."

Nicola grabbed a long black velvet cloak and waved her hand. "Maybe, but you can bet plenty of women have thought it. You look great in a tux. Now stop fishing for compliments and help me with my cloak. It's a little chilly out there tonight, isn't it?"

"It's chilly outside, but the limo is warm," he said as he helped her into her cloak. It was a damn shame to cover her the way she looked tonight. It made a lot more sense to uncover her inch by luscious inch. Her green dress draped over her shoulders offering an enticing view of her ample cleavage. Nicola's body had always driven him nuts. Despite her complaints that she could lose fifteen pounds, Abe knew she had curves in all the right places.

He led her to the limo and she sat in the center of one seat. Struggling with an itch to be closer to her, he sat perpendicular. "Would you like a drink? I have your favorite wine."

He glimpsed a quick shot of longing in her eyes then she set her chin and shook her head. "Just water tonight." She pulled her PalmPilot from her small evening bag. "Let's review who will be attending the ball tonight."

She coached and quizzed him during the entire drive to the governor's mansion. "I think you're ready," she said as the driver stopped in front of the entrance.

Abe escorted her inside and he was struck by an odd feeling. Nicola had attended many events with him, but tonight felt different. She might see it as a business function and he'd had to wrap it that way to persuade her to join him, but for Abe, he just wanted her company. He wanted to be close enough to hear her laughter.

"There's our reelected congressman. You should say hello."

And so it went for the next hour. With Nicola watching the crowd to make sure Abe didn't miss speaking to anyone, Abe felt almost as if he was back on the campaign trail again. The only difference was that he didn't say, "I hope you'll vote for me." Instead he said, "Thank you for supporting me."

Dinner was announced, offering him a quick breather.

"Thank goodness for dinner," Nicola said as she and Abe stepped to the side. "What a crush that was. I should have expected it, though."

"Why should you have expected it? I didn't," he said, adjusting his tie.

Nicola smiled at him. "Because you're so popular that *everyone* wants a chance to talk to you."

Abe rolled his eyes. "Careful. You're starting to believe the PR you wrote for me."

"Which was the truth," she retorted. "I guess we should go in for dinner."

He offered her his arm. "You better be seated beside me."

She whirled her head to look at him. "You know that's not going to happen. We've never been seated together before."

"That was different," he said, feeling irritated that he couldn't have Nicola to himself. "That was during the campaign."

"Well, even though this looks social, it's still a political function. You'll be at one table and I'll be at another. Remember you're an important and fascinating senator, and I'm unimportant, boring staff."

His irritation climbed another notch. "That's bull. You couldn't be less boring." He stopped and looked at her so she wouldn't miss his point. "And you're a helluva lot more than staff."

Her eyes widened and color rose to her cheeks. "We need to move on. People are starting to look at us."

Although he knew he would always have to account for his actions because he was in public office, he was growing impatient with being concerned about what others might think of his relationship with Nicola.

"Nic, we need to talk," Abe began.

He would have sworn he glimpsed a trace of panic on her face, but she glanced away. "Oh, look there's the governor, and he's headed straight for you, Senator."

* * *

An hour and a half later, Abe glanced in Nicola's direction for the tenth time. She'd been right. He had been seated at the governor's table and Nicola had been seated several tables away. The prime rib had tasted better than most banquet fare and the woman seated on his right had managed to drop into the conversation no less than five times that she was widowed. Nicola, he noticed, was seated between two men treating her as if she were roast tenderloin and they hadn't had a meal in a month.

The band started playing and Abe saw Nicola laugh and shake her head as one of the men pointed toward the dance floor. Abe felt a sliver of relief when she shook her head again.

"You look like a man who would be excellent on his feet." Vivian, the woman beside him interrupted his watch over Nicola. "Would you like to dance?"

Not really, he thought and swallowed his refusal. The woman had been an active generous supporter of his campaign. Abe knew his attitude sucked. He was going to have to fix it. "My pleasure," he said, standing and extending his hand.

He escorted Vivian to the floor and nodded as she discussed her garden club. "We would love to visit Crofthaven in the spring. Is there any chance?"

"My housekeeper and assistant make those decisions. As you know Crofthaven has a few years on her, so it seems like we're always renovating something."

The song ended and the band struck up a faster tune.

Vivian smiled and shook her head. "Speaking of having a few years, this song is too young for my blood. What about you?"

Abe nodded and offered his arm to escort Vivian back to the table. Just as he turned, he saw Nicola dancing with *both* of the men from her table. He blinked. She laughed as she shimmied and danced.

"We can leave that kind of dancing for the young crowd," Vivian said, taking her seat. "Would you like some more wine?"

No, Abe thought. *I'd like a Scotch. Make it a double.*

"Didn't I read that one of your children is getting married soon?" Vivian asked.

"Yes. Adam and Selene." He noticed the music slowed down a couple of notches and one of the young men dancing with Nicola pulled her into his arms. Abe's gut and throat tightened. He tugged at his collar.

"That must have presented an awkward situation for you. Your son getting romantically involved with your opponent's daughter."

Abe couldn't contain his irritation any longer. "Not at all. Selene's a lovely girl and she and Adam make each other very happy. That's what really matters, isn't it?" he said, then rose to his feet. "Excuse me."

He didn't know if he was more irritated with Vivian's references to his age or Nicola dancing so closely with the young turk from her dinner table. He couldn't do a damn thing about his age, but he could do something about Nicola. Approaching the dancing couple, he tapped the man on his shoulder. "May I?"

Nicola looked at him in surprise, her partner looked at him in confusion. "May you what?" her partner asked.

"May I cut in?" Abe ordered more than asked.

"Oh, sure. Sure." The young man smiled. "Go ahead. I'll catch you later, Nicola."

Abe swallowed a growl and pulled Nicola into his arms. "Those two moved in fast," he said, sighing at the sensation of her body against his. It had been too long.

"What?"

"Your dinner companions," he said, unable to keep the irritation from his tone.

"Harmless flirts. I figured I was lucky I didn't get stuck next to someone boring."

"Like I did," Abe muttered.

Nicola looked up at him. "Is that why you cut in to dance with me? To rescue yourself from boredom?"

"You can think that if you want," he said, stroking the inside of her wrist with his thumb.

She bit her lip. "What a noncommittal response, Senator."

"You want committed? I can give you committed," Abe said, guiding her to a less crowded area. "I'm tired of pretending there's nothing between us. I'm tired of playing games with the press and the public. I'm tired of you playing games with me."

Her mouth rounded in surprise. "What do you mean? I haven't been playing games with you."

"Damn right you have. Every step I take toward you, you take one back. So, what is it, Nic? Do you think I'm too old for you or not? Do you want me or not?"

She gasped. "I never ever said you were too old. You were always the one to harp on that."

"So you don't have a problem with my age," he said crisply.

"No." She glanced from side to side, then back at him. "Your maturity and experience have always been a turn-on for me. I've always been drawn to how decisive you are," she added grudgingly.

The tension inside him eased a millimeter. "Then it all comes down to what we want. I want you, Nic. I want you bad, and I don't give a damn who knows it. The question is whether you want me or not."

Nicola closed her eyes. "You're not making it easy for me to do the right thing."

"What's the right thing, Nic? Letting our chance to be together slip away because I'm an elected official?"

She inhaled shakily and opened her eyes. "You're not making this easy for me at all," she repeated.

Abe saw the wanting written in her eyes, but he wanted her to admit it. He wanted to hear it. Needed to hear it. "I can make it a lot easier," he said, lowering his head.

"You're not going to kiss me in front of all these people," she whispered, her eyes wide with shock.

"Watch me."

Nicola acted out of pure damage-control instincts. She turned her head and Abe's mouth landed on her cheek.

He squeezed her shoulders and chuckled next to her ear. "You stinker. I would never have taken you for a chicken."

Her head shot up, her ego pinched by his accusation. "I'm not a chicken."

"Do you want me?" he asked her in a silky, sexy voice that slid through her like fine wine.

She struggled against his effect on her. "I told you it's not always about what I want."

"In this case it can be about what you want, Nic, because I sure as hell want you."

Nicola gulped at the heat in his eyes and the rock-hard decisiveness in his voice. She'd heard him use that tone before, but never with her name in the subject line.

"Think about what you want, Nic," he said as he stroked the bare skin of her arm. It was a hidden intimate touch that made her breath uneven. "This party will be over soon enough."

An odd lump in her throat kept all her snappy rejections from popping out. Abe led her back to her seat and nodded to the rest of the people at the table. "Later," he said to her and her heart hiccupped. *Later* could mean so many things.

She'd never seen Abe so serious about her before. Maybe his feelings ran deeper than she'd assumed. Maybe he wanted more than the secret affair they'd alternated between giving in to and squashing. Maybe he almost loved her.

Her heart hammered in her chest and she felt her blood rise to her cheeks. Her mind raced with all the possibilities she'd disciplined herself to never consider. What if he actually grew to *love* her? What if he wanted them to be together all the time? Married? Could he come to terms with the baby? Her stomach twisted at that thought. She absolutely didn't want to spend her life trying to get Abe to love their child. She couldn't do it.

She glanced across the room at him and he must have felt her looking at him because he returned her gaze boldly. As if he didn't care who might see him looking at her that way.

Her heart skipped a beat and her doubtful mind bounced up and down with hope. If he could change his mind about wanting to have a public relationship with her, then maybe he could change his mind about other things, too.

After the ball, Nicola joined Abe in the limo for the ride to the hotel. They discussed the various political contacts Abe and Nicola had made throughout the evening. Underneath it all, however, Nicola felt a hum of anticipation between them. The driver had already checked them in, their overnight luggage was waiting in their rooms. She and Abe arrived at their respective rooms, placed side by side.

"Hope you like your room," he said, and surprised her by going inside his room.

He hadn't even tried to kiss her, she thought, surprised and a little disappointed. She shouldn't be disappointed, she told herself as she opened her door and stepped inside. If he was going to be so up and down about this, then she didn't need— Her mental ranting broke off when she realized theirs were connecting rooms and the doors were open.

That devil. That dog. Abe stood in the connecting room doorway, tugging loose his tux tie. "Does this suit you better? Since you don't want to be seen with an old fart like me?"

Nicola wanted to slap that sexy grin off his face. Or kiss him. Unable to choke down her chuckle, she laughed and met him in the doorway. She poked her finger at his hard chest. "You're the most ridiculous man in the world," she said. "Old fart? Nowhere near."

He captured her hand and held it against his chest. "I figured that was the only reason you wouldn't want to be seen with me."

Nicola sighed. "I told you it's to protect your image."

"I don't need to protect my image that way anymore, Nic. What about you?"

Her breath felt tight in her chest. "I think you know

it was never about image with me. The more I got to know you, the more I—" Her throat went dry and she swallowed.

"The more you what?" he prompted.

"The more I wanted to be with you," she whispered.

"You keep using past tense. What about now, Nic?" he asked, lifting her hand to his mouth.

This could be a perfect escape, a temporary escape, the little voice of survival inside her prompted. She could say her feelings had changed. She could say she didn't feel the same way about him anymore, that he no longer had the power to make her heart stop and start with just a look, that she didn't dream about being in his arms every night. She could say that she didn't want him. Nicola opened her mouth, but the words stuck in her throat.

"No answer, but your eyes are talking. Maybe I need to ask the question a different way," he said and lowered his head.

This time his mouth took hers, and oh, he felt so good. The way he kissed her, sensually plucking at her mouth with his lips, made her feel as if she were a rosebud. Nicola swallowed a moan.

He slid his fingers through her hair and gently caressed her scalp as he tilted her head for better access. Nicola felt her skin grow hot and she was caught between the mind-drugging sensation of his fingertips on her scalp and the desire to deepen the kiss.

He deepened it for her, sliding his tongue inside and tasting her. He gave a low moan that vibrated through her nether regions. He gently consumed her mouth, making her feel like the most desirable woman in the world. The taste of his want made her light-headed.

Unable to stifle her response to him, she reveled in the strength of his shoulders and craved the feeling of his bare skin against hers. Her mouth still fastened to his, she blindly unfastened his shirt. He gave a low growl of approval.

She pulled away from him, gulping in a breath of air while her heart hammered against her rib cage. "You make it so difficult to resist you."

"Thank goodness I've got something on my side," he muttered, tugging off his undershirt. "Do you have any idea how hard it was for me to watch those two guys trying to charm you out of your dress? Add their ages together and you'll get mine."

Nicola couldn't resist a breathless chuckle. "They weren't trying to charm me out of my dress," she protested.

He rolled his eyes. "Nic, you can be incredibly naive about your appeal."

"And what's with the constant senior citizen remarks? Just trust me when I tell you those guys don't have one-tenth of your virility." Nicola could guarantee that fact. She had the evidence in her womb.

Abe stopped and let out a breath of air, his gaze full of turbulence. "I want more than a night with you, Nic.

I want more than a secret affair. I want a relationship and I don't mean a working relationship."

Nicola's heart felt as if it had stopped in her chest. "What are you talking about?"

He took her hand. "I'm crazy about you," he said in a voice brimming with impatience and a sliver of anger.

"You don't sound very happy about it."

"I'm still working on it. I hadn't planned on this— you—happening right now. The way I feel about you, it's not convenient. But I can't turn it off. It's too strong. Even though I'm too old for you, I can't let you go."

Nicola felt light-headed again, but she couldn't blame Abe's kiss. This time it was his words. The intensity in his eyes thrilled her and frightened her. She still needed to tell him about the baby. "You're making me dizzy. I need to sit down for a minute."

Before she could blink, he picked her up and carried her to her bed. "Oh, no! You're going to hurt your back or get a hernia and it will be my fault!"

Abe followed her down on the bed. "Quit exaggerating. You're the perfect size and I can prove it," he said, pulling her against him.

"Don't kiss me. I need time to think," she protested.

"I don't want you to think too much. That could be bad for me."

She felt him unzip her zipper and one second later, her strapless bra was unfastened. "Oh, Abe, we really shouldn't—"

He slid his hands to her breasts and her mouth couldn't produce anything but a sound of pleasure. Her breasts seemed more sensitive than usual.

He lightly touched the sides, drawing circles with his fingers that came close but didn't quite touch her nipples. "You want me to stop?"

"Ohhh, that's sooo—" She bit her lip as he rubbed his thumb over one nipple.

"Good?" he asked, lowering his mouth to hers.

"Yes." She felt as if every nerve ending inside her was buzzing. Her breasts grew heavy with arousal.

Sucking gently on her tongue, he tugged at her nipples and Nicola felt a corresponding bloom between her legs. Her nipples grew stiff from his caresses.

"Oh, Abe, you feel—"

"I can make you feel better," he promised and lowered his mouth to one of her nipples. He licked and suckled, making her squirm beneath him. She loved the way his big hands felt on her. Inhaling the subtle scent of his aftershave, she felt her arousal rise with shocking speed.

When he pulled back slightly she couldn't withhold a moan. "Don't stop, pl—"

He transferred his wonderful, wicked mouth to her other nipple while still caressing the one he'd just suckled with his thumb and forefinger. He drew deeply and the restlessness between her thighs increased. He continued his mesmerizing caresses and she felt the tension in her nether regions draw into a knot. Her heart pounded and she couldn't lie still. He gave her a super sensual nip followed by sucking her deep into his mouth and Nicola shocked herself by climaxing.

Catching her breath, she gaped in amazement. Was this due to her pregnancy? Had she read something about this in her pregnancy book? Her head was a fog and her body was still shimmering with pleasure. "Uh, that was uh—" She stared into Abe's sexy gaze.

Abe's eyes crinkled with sexy humor. "That was a nice surprise," he said in a low, deep voice of approval that melted her bones. "Very nice. Now if I can get you out of the rest of your clothes, I'd like to do some mo—"

A vibrating sound coming from his pocket stopped him. He glanced down. The vibration sounded again. Clearly conflicted, he met Nicola's gaze. "Damn, life was easier before these were invented. I should at least check who—" He pulled out his cell phone and glanced at the caller ID. "It's Marc. I have to take it." He gave her a quick, firm kiss full of promise. "Don't go anywhere."

"As if I could," she managed.

Six

Twenty minutes later, Abe turned off his cell phone and headed back to Nicola. He couldn't wait to tell her the news about Marc. He couldn't wait to gorge himself on her body. He was still aroused by how she'd responded to him. He strode toward her bed and found her fast asleep. She'd shimmied out of her dress and draped it over her chair. With her shoulders bare, he suspected she was naked beneath the sheet. She'd left her bedside lamp on, probably full of intention to remain awake.

He sighed and raked his hand through his hair. She looked exhausted and he would be a caveman to wake her and take her. But heaven help him, the woman made him feel like a caveman.

Pounding sexual need warred with the voice of his conscience. The woman was worn out. Closing his eyes, he inhaled and slowly exhaled. There would be other times, he promised himself and turned off the bedside lamp.

Nicola awakened early the next morning. She immediately rolled to her side expecting to see Abe, but he wasn't there. Frowning, she stretched, trying to remember what had happened after she'd brushed her teeth, lain down and waited for him to join her in bed. She remembered feeling exhausted and trying with all her might to keep her eyelids open.

It looked as if she'd flunked that endurance test, she thought, chagrined. She heard a knock on Abe's door and a low murmur. Catching the scents of coffee and bacon, she felt her stomach turn.

His hair damp from a shower, Abe appeared in the inner doorway between their rooms. "Ready for some breakfast, sleepyhead? I ordered enough for two."

She swallowed a surge of nausea. "Thanks. I must have overindulged on last night's dinner. I don't feel very hungry right now. Maybe some toast?"

With one hand hitched through a belt loop, he loped into the room and grinned down at her. "I still feel hungry this morning."

Nicola could tell from his expression that he wasn't talking about food. She winced. "I'm sorry I fell asleep. I guess I was more tired…and more satisfied than I realized."

He sank down on her bed and lifted his hand to her cheek. "I want to continue now, but we need to get back to celebrate with Marc and Dana. They've caught the members of the cartel who were trying to frame him."

Nicola gasped and lifted up on her elbows. "Oh, that's wonderful. I know they're thrilled. I know *you're* thrilled."

"It's great news. I would have told you last night, but you were out like a light." He tweaked her nose. "Rain check?"

She nodded, but wasn't sure a rain check would be wise.

He extended his hand. "Join me for breakfast."

Nicola's stomach felt tenuous at best. She smiled. "You get started and let me take a superquick shower. Okay?"

His lifted eyebrow emanated doubt. "Superquick? Women and bathing rarely equal superquick."

She swatted at him playfully. "Don't be sexist." She tossed aside her covers and slowly slid out of the bed, trying to cover her light-headedness.

Abe reached from behind her and slid his hand over her bare belly. "Are you sure I can't help?" he murmured.

"Stop sabotaging me. There's no way I'll get out of that shower superquick if you're in there with me."

Abe gave a sexy groan. "Oh, Nic, someday soon, I'm turning off my cell phone and I'm spending the entire day in bed with you."

He kissed her neck and Nicola wondered if she could match his stamina for an entire day in bed.

* * *

That afternoon, several members of the Danforth family gathered for an impromptu celebration for Marc and Dana. Dom Pérignon flowed freely among the crowd and Abe lifted his glass in a toast. "To Marc and Dana, a great team in life and love. May your toughest battle be over and only joy and pleasure ahead." He clicked his glass with Marc and Dana, then gently clicked it with Nicola's glass.

Meeting his gaze over the rim of her flute, she took the tiniest sip. "Here, here," she said, feeling light-headed at the intent expression on his face. He'd been so attentive today she could almost think they had a future. Almost.

She'd been a bundle of nerves since this morning, unable to eat anything except toast and crackers, which she'd munched throughout the day. Even now she felt a little woozy.

"Nic," Abe said as if he was repeating himself. "Are you okay?"

She tried to take a deep breath, but the room was spinning. "I'm fine. I just feel a little dizzy." Her knees lost their starch and she tried in vain to stiffen them. To her chagrin, she felt herself fall.

Abe caught her, whispering an oath. "What's going on here? You're pale as a ghost."

"Nicola!"

"Nicola?"

She heard the concern in several voices, but a black curtain fell over her.

Nicola was mortified. She'd never fainted in her life. Now Abe had tucked her into her former room and was ranting and raving, twisting the arm of the family doctor to visit.

"It's not necessary," she said, ignoring his shushing finger. She started to rise from the bed and he was by her side in seconds.

"Don't even think about it," he said to her, then turned his attention back to his phone. "Ten minutes. Thank you for coming right over, Dr. Bernard." He clicked the phone off.

"This is ridiculous," she said, boosting her pillow so she wasn't flat on her back. It didn't help her argument that he was looming over her. "I'm fine. I just got a little light-headed because I didn't eat enough earlier." She supposed she should have eaten more than crackers, but nothing substantial had appealed to her.

"Then we'll fix that right after the doctor leaves," Abe said. "And I'll stay here to watch you eat every bite."

"My stomach hasn't felt great today," she confessed. "Maybe it's a virus," she fibbed, then shot him a dark look. "Maybe you'll catch it because you kissed me."

Abe shrugged. "I never get sick."

Nicola rolled her eyes. "Don't rub it in. You'll make this mere mortal woman feel worse."

Looking down at her, he stood beside the bed with his hands on his hips and sighed. "I don't like seeing you sick."

Good thing he hadn't seen her those times she'd glued herself to the sofa until the room stopped moving. "I'm sure it's not fatal. Just a little bug, if that."

He scratched the back of his neck. "Come to think of it, you've looked a little pale lately. Maybe you should make an appointment to get your blood checked."

Nicola bit her lip. Wouldn't that be just what she needed? A blood test and Abe would, of course, demand to see the results. "I just had it checked during my annual checkup and I'm perfectly normal."

"We'll see," he said, glancing at his watch. "Can I get you anything to drink or eat?"

She still didn't feel like eating, but knew she had to eat for the baby. "Maybe just a little chicken noodle soup and some crackers."

He nodded. "Done." She watched him punch the intercom button and give the housekeeper the order. Just as he finished, a knock sounded at the door. Abe opened the door. "Dr. Bernard. You're here in record time."

"You sounded worried," said the sixty-plus-year-old man with a gray mustache and kind face. He glanced in Nicola's direction. "What seems to be the problem?"

"She fainted dead away while we were toasting Marc and Dana. She says she hasn't eaten much and her stomach hasn't felt well for several days."

The doctor sat on the bed next to her. "Do you mind?" he asked, putting his fingers on her wrist and looking at his watch.

"Not at all," Nicola said. "But I didn't faint dead away. I just got dizzy and blacked out for less than a second."

"Let me check your blood pressure," Dr. Bernard said.

"She would have fallen to the floor if I hadn't caught her," Abe said. "Could've ended up with a concussion."

"There you go. Exaggerating again," Nicola retorted.

"You didn't see how pale you were," Abe said.

"Abe, leave the room. You're disturbing the patient."

Abe's jaw dropped in surprise. Nicola stifled the urge to laugh. Abe was accustomed to giving orders, not taking them.

"I mean it, Abe. I need to examine Miss Granville without distraction and your presence is affecting her blood pressure."

Abe opened his mouth then shut it. His eyes lit with a sliver of amusement. "Good to know I affect her blood pressure."

The doctor chuckled as Abe walked out the door. "What a rascal. I hope you know what you're in for."

"What do you mean?" Nicola asked.

"I mean Abe Danforth usually gets what he wants and it looks like you are what he wants. Tell me a little more about these symptoms. You look a little pale. Did you drink alcohol on an empty stomach?"

"Half a sip. I'm not a big drinker. I'll be fine. This is temporary."

Dr. Bernard studied her face over his glasses. "You sound awfully confident. How long have you been nauseated?"

"Off and on for a couple of weeks, but it doesn't last long."

He frowned. "We could do a couple of blood tests—"

"Not necessary. I just had a checkup and I'm fine," she insisted, wishing the good doctor wasn't quite so thorough.

"Hmm," he said, lifting her chin and studying her. "Have you been running a fever?"

She shook her head. "No. See? Nothing serious. Abe is just overreacting."

"Overprotective," Dr. Bernard corrected. "He's always been big on protecting what's important to him." He cleared his throat. "There are several causes of nausea. Have you had a pregnancy test?"

Nicola blinked, a denial stuck in her throat.

"If you have taken a pregnancy test and it was positive, then you need to make sure you're eating well for your nutrition and the baby's."

Nicola bit her lip in panic. What if Dr. Bernard told Abe… She just wasn't ready to deal with Abe's response, whatever it might be.

Dr. Bernard touched her palms which had grown damp. "Have you told the baby's father?"

Unable to lie, Nicola gave a minute shake of her head. "Please don't tell him."

Dr. Bernard nodded. "I won't, but you should," he said, rising from the bed. "Are you taking your vitamins?"

"Absolutely," she said, sagging in relief.

"Good. Stay hydrated and eat when you can. Rest when you can't eat. Don't wait too long to tell Abe. These things have a way of getting out."

Nicola nodded. Good advice, she thought, but *how?*

Abe insisted Nicola stay the night and joined her in her room while they watched Jimmy Stewart in *It's A Wonderful Life,* and she sipped chicken noodle soup.

"Another bite," he encouraged.

She smiled and shook her head. "What are you going to do next? Pretend my spoon is an airplane and fly it into my mouth?"

"If it'll work," he said and took the spoon from her. "Open the hangar so the plane can fly inside."

Nicola laughed and he fed her a spoonful of soup. "You make me feel like a five-year-old."

"Trust me. You don't feel like a five-year-old to me," he said, his eyes dark and sensual.

Nicola's pulse picked up at his expression. "I wonder, if you hadn't been busy conquering the world, what you would have been like as a father."

Abe's smile fell. "I'd like to think I would have done things differently."

Her heart raced. Was this the right moment? "If you had the chance now, do you think you would?"

His eyes widened. "Have a child now?" He chuckled in disbelief. "I'm old enough for grandchildren. I don't have any business having more children. I'll just hope that my children will allow me to enjoy my grandchildren every now and then." He paused and glanced at her. "What about you? I've always gotten the impression you've been as focused on your career as I have. No time for kids. Any regrets?"

"I don't know anyone who doesn't have regrets," she hedged, backing off because the moment didn't feel quite so right after all. "But you're right. I've been so busy with my career that I haven't had time to think about having children."

"Feel your clock ticking?" he asked.

She swallowed nervous laughter. "Not lately."

"What about marriage? I haven't met a woman yet who hasn't dreamed of white lace and the perfect groom at some time in her life."

A bittersweet memory stole across her mind. She'd been deeply infatuated with her high school sweetheart and had been so sure they would marry. She'd been so wrong. "That was a long time ago for me. There's no such thing as the perfect groom. I've learned that men can cause complications. They can bail at the worst possible moment. Better not to depend on them."

"Sounds like you had a rough experience," he said quietly.

"Most people have been bumped around a little romantically speaking by the time they get out of college. Maybe you wouldn't know because you always got the girl," she teased. "Although I thought I heard you once say you worked hard to win your wife." She made a tsk-ing sound. "Always had to have a challenge."

He tossed her a sideways glance and groaned. "I hope I've grown a little since then. You're right. My wife was the debutante of the season. At least three of us were competing for her. The day she said yes I felt like I'd won an endurance contest."

"Why do you think she said yes?"

He turned serious and looked away, narrowing his eyes. "Truth?"

She nodded.

"I think she wanted Crofthaven."

His response shocked her. "Oh, it had to be more than that. I'm sure she was in love with you."

Abe shrugged. "We were both very young, and selfish the way young people can be. She was my prize and Crofthaven was her palace." He met her gaze. "Neither of us ended up being happy. My marriage doesn't provide a great recommendation for romantic relationships."

"That depends," Nicola said.

"On what?"

"On whether you learned anything from it," she said. "And if you've changed."

He lifted his hand to her cheek. "And what have you learned from your experiences with men?"

"Not to count on them," she said. "And not to let them take over my life."

"Committed to your independence," he mused.

She had been. Until now, she thought, putting a hand over her womb and thinking of the baby.

Abe covered her hand with his. "Stomach still upset?"

She shook her head and met his gaze. "No. I think I must have been running on pure adrenaline during those last weeks of the campaign. My body's just reacting to the letdown." With Abe close to her and his hand on hers, she felt oddly vulnerable and protected at the same time. She bit her lip.

"We've spent almost the entire past year together and I feel like I barely know you," Abe said.

"We were busy with strategies and politics. We didn't have time."

He nodded. "We have time now, though, Nic."

Not much, she thought, her stomach drawing into a knot. Not much time at all.

Just two nights later after the rehearsal dinner for Adam and Selene's wedding, Abe invited the men into his study for a shot of excellent Scotch before his sons and a few of Adam's friends took off for Adam's last night as a bachelor.

Adam was reluctant. "If you guys get me in trouble with Selene, I promise to make your life a living hell."

Ian grinned. "Go ahead and try, bro. You don't have anything to worry about. We have women we have to answer to, too."

Adam shook his head. "I'd rather try to get a few more quiet moments with Selene before chaos hits tomorrow."

"Chaos has already hit, my man," Ian said. "The women are hitting the town tonight, too."

Adam's eyes widened. "They're taking Selene out? I thought she was going home so she'd get plenty of rest for tomorrow."

"She probably thought that, too," Ian said and chuckled. "But I have it on good authority that she's being kidnapped and taken to a place where half-naked men dance and serve drinks."

Abe couldn't withhold a laugh at the sick expression on Adam's face. He clapped him on the shoulder. "Don't worry. Selene's just as crazy for you as you are for her. I'm sure they won't let her get too wild."

Adam tossed back his Scotch. "This is great," he said, disgusted. "Just great."

"I'm sure your comrades will help you forget your worries." Abe lifted his glass and spoke from his heart and sadder, but wiser experience. "To Adam, a great brother and friend, a son I'm tremendously proud of.

Cherish your wife and love her well. Stay by her side and you'll both be happy."

He looked at each of his sons and saw one more millimeter of acceptance in their eyes. They nodded and murmured in agreement then downed their whiskey.

"Time to hit the road, Adam," his other brother Reid said.

"Okay, okay," Adam said and lowered his voice as he spoke to Abe. "Thanks. Better stay on your toes yourself, Dad. I think I overheard Jasmine saying she wanted to set up Nicola with some guy she interviewed for a story."

Abe's mouth suddenly tasted bitter. Jasmine was married to Wes Brooks, a longtime family friend. "With friends like these…" Abe muttered.

Seven

The following day Abe watched Adam kiss his bride after the minister pronounced them man and wife. At the reception, Abe toasted the couple and watched them lead the first dance. An odd emotion twisted in his chest as the music and the crowd swam around him in the beautifully decorated ballroom.

He remembered the day Adam had been born. Abe hadn't even been in the country. When Abe had returned and held his tiny son in his arms, he'd felt proud and humbled by the responsibility. He'd always wanted his children to have every advantage. He'd wanted his children to be proud of their father.

Regret burned in his stomach. He absently rubbed at

his gut and caught a whiff of a familiar spicy perfume. Nicola. Standing beside him, she smiled, and something inside him eased.

"How's the father of the groom doing?" she asked.

"This is a little tougher than I anticipated," he said, adjusting his tie.

"A little choked up?" she asked, her eyes gentle.

"Yeah." The fragrance of the mounds of red and white roses throughout the room got to him. He shook his head. "I need some air. Join me?"

She hesitated only a second then nodded. "Sure."

He led her onto the screened terrace of the hotel's ballroom, welcoming the chilly blast of air. Catching her take a quick breath, he pulled off his jacket. "Here, take this."

"I'm fine," she protested, but pulled his jacket around her. "But this does feel nice and warm." She put her hand on his arm. "Are you okay?"

He shoved his hands into his pockets and nodded. "Just thinking about how many years passed that I wasn't there for them."

Nicola was quiet for a moment and the strains of a romantic melody playing inside the ballroom filtered onto the terrace. "I know it hurts," Nicola said. "You can think about what you've missed or make the best of the present and future."

"You're awfully wise for such a young woman," he said, looking into her eyes. The more he was with her, the more he wanted to be with her.

She rolled her eyes. "I'm not that young."

He reached for her and pulled her against him. "Now that's pure hogwash," he said, swaying to the music.

She tried not to smile, but failed. "There's no such thing as *pure* hogwash, and are you dancing with me?"

He nodded. "Just following your advice. You said I should make the best of the present and the future. I'm on a terrace alone with a woman who takes my breath away. I'm making the best of the present."

She closed her eyes and leaned her forehead against his chin. "You shouldn't say those things."

"Why not? They're true. You know me. Honest Abe, the last honest politician in America."

"I don't believe I take your breath away," she said.

"Then you haven't been paying attention." He brushed his mouth over the top of her head and wondered how he was going to convince Nicola to come to D.C. with him.

The evening wore on and the time arrived for the tossing of the bouquet. Abe watched the wild jockeying for position. He spotted Jasmine trying to drag Nicola into the fray, but Nic kept shaking her head. He stepped closer to hear what they were saying.

"C'mon, Nicola, be a good sport. We've got just about everyone else hooked up. Why not you?"

"Because I'm strictly single. I'm not getting married."

"Why not?" Jasmine asked, still trying to coax Nicola to the bouquet-catching group.

"Because men aren't worth the hassle."

"You just haven't met the right one," Jasmine continued.

"I've met all the right ones and they're still not right for me," Nicola said.

"But—"

The bouquet went sailing through the air and landed at Nicola's feet. Wearing a look of exasperation, she gave the bouquet a gentle shove with her foot. "Live bouquet," she called. "Better grab it before the referee calls it dead."

A melee of women diving for the bouquet ensued with Nic scrambling to get out of the way. Abe's brother, Harold, stepped beside him and chuckled. "I always thought there was something primitive about that bouquet tossing. The tossing part is okay. It's the catching that looks—"

"—like a train wreck," Abe said, wondering how many stockings would be ruined, how many fingernails left on the floor. A smiling woman with her hair mussed and a smudge on her face finally stood and lifted the bouquet up high as if it was a trophy.

"Do you think they really believe it?" Abe asked.

"I think it's like fate giving you an extra boost. And look at Nicola, standing back from it all as if she wants nothing to do with it, the bouquet or the wedding."

"Sure looks that way," Abe said, the notion bothering him for some reason he couldn't name. He'd prefer she be at least open to the idea of marriage. For her it was clearly a closed subject.

"This reminds me of how hard you chased Chloe. She was the one everyone wanted and you got her."

Abe nodded. "She was the only woman I ever courted."

"You haven't had to since then. They come to you."

Not the one he wanted. He watched Nicola smiling and shaking her head, and it hit him. If he wanted Nicola, he was going to have to court her. In order to court her, he would need to know her favorites. His first wife, Chloe, had practically broadcasted her favorites, so that her boyfriends always knew to bring her red roses and fine milk chocolates.

Abe only knew a few of Nicola's favorites—her favorite white wine, which she hadn't been drinking lately, steak prepared medium, herbal tea, crackers and Skittles when she was nervous. She wore clothes that celebrated her womanly shape and favored soft blankets and comfortable furnishings.

If he had more information, he could use a more targeted approach. Instead, he would have to use the spaghetti-toss method. Throw the spaghetti and see what sticks.

"I've been given two tickets to *The Nutcracker.* Come with me," he said the following afternoon.

She glanced up from the list she'd been compiling. "Was that an invitation or an order?"

"An invitation, of course. Would you like that?"

"I'm not big on ballet, but I've always wanted to see *The Nutcracker* live. It will put me in the Christmas spirit."

"Speaking of Christmas, you do plan to join us at Crofthaven, don't you? We're all expecting you."

"I don't know. I was thinking I might have a quiet Christmas this year."

"Can I join you?" he asked in a conspiratorial voice.

Nicola chuckled. "You can't mean that."

"Yes, I can," Abe said. "You wouldn't mind if I stayed with you for a few nights, would you? You could just think of it as rescuing me."

Nicola laughed again. "You're nuts. And I have a hard time believing you need to be rescued from anything."

He moved closer and crouched down in front of her. "There's this woman who is driving me crazy. I think I'm going to need some help to get through to her."

She bit her lip and her eyes darkened. "What do you want from this woman?"

"Not much," he said, sliding his hand over her knee. "Just every minute of every day, her undivided attention, her mind, body and heart."

Nicola's eyes widened. "You don't ask for much, do you? What are you offering in return? Can you offer every minute of every day, your undivided attention, your mind, body and heart?"

Abe fell silent. The woman had a point. He was asking for a helluva lot. Exactly what was he willing to give in return? "Good question. You've always been too intelligent."

"Abe, haven't you heard not to ask for what you're not willing to give?"

"Yes, I have, but I've never applied it to romantic relationships. I never batted an eye going into life-threatening situations with fellow SEALs because I knew I would give up my life if necessary and they would do the same."

"I hear it's different when deciding where to go for dinner, what color to wallpaper the walls and who gets which section of the paper first. Or who's going to get up in the middle of the night when the baby is crying and change the messy diaper."

"I did change some messy diapers," he told her.

"In the middle of the night?"

"We had a nanny for that." He met her gaze. She'd given him something to think about. Nicola often did that to him. That ability to make him think and reflect was part of what fascinated and frustrated him about her. For now, he had to get some other questions answered. "What did you think of all the red and white roses at Adam and Selene's wedding?"

"They were beautiful and a nice tie-in for Christmas," Nicola said.

"What are you favorites?"

"Flowers?" She shrugged. "I love the mixed bouquets with unusual colored roses and other flowers. I'm not a straight red-rose kind of girl."

"What about the wedding cake?"

"That was gorgeous, amazing. Black and white, chocolate and vanilla to suit both tastes. Very clever."

"My favorite is Boston cream pie," he said.

"Really? I would've guessed apple. You ordered it so often during the campaign."

"Apple is my second favorite."

"My favorite cake is Mississippi Mud, not at all appropriate for a wedding, but that's okay because when I make it, I don't like to share it."

He laughed. "You selfish little thing. How often do you make it?"

"About once a year. Otherwise, it's—"

"—Skittles," he finished for her, enjoying the look of surprise on her face.

"And you're a mint or antacid cruncher, depending on whether or not you overindulged in barbecue."

"You're too observant," he told her.

"Maybe, but I am observing that we've gotten off track here. What's next on the list?"

"Gifts for the Angel Tree, but I can give that to my—"

"No, no. I love that. I have to shop for two of my angels myself. How many did you get?"

"Ten," Abe said and watched her eyes widen.

"Ten?" she echoed.

"I told you that I can give that assignment to my assistant."

She shook her head. "Is this what you do every year? Pull ten of these off a tree and give your assistant the money to go buy the gifts."

He shrugged. "Yes. Ten seemed a fair number in light of the other holiday donations I give."

"Oh, ten is very generous," Nicola said. "Ever thought about doing the shopping yourself?"

Not in a million years, he thought, but caught himself before he said it aloud. "Not until now. Will you help me?"

"You would actually go out in the mass of humanity and go shopping for your Christmas angels?" she asked, incredulous.

"I will if you will," he said.

At Nicola's suggestion, they went to Wal-Mart at midnight. Abe glanced around in amazement at the number of shoppers in the store. "I didn't know Wal-Mart was open past midnight."

"All night until Christmas," Nicola said with a grim smile. "You can shop here twenty-four hours a day if you want."

Abe shuddered. "Sounds like a nightmare to me."

"The reason we came at midnight is because neither you nor I like to wait in line, and due to all the crowds we dealt with during the campaign, we'd like a little break from hordes of people."

"Smart woman," Abe said in approval, wondering if they could speed shop and then he could get her home to her town house and join her in bed. "Where are the lists?"

"Here," she said. "You do the boy toys. I'll do the clothing and girl toys."

"Okay, when I get done with mine, I can help you with yours."

They went their separate ways and Abe selected the toys for the boys. He threw in a few extras that looked like fun then went looking for Nicola and found her in the infant department looking at baby clothes and baby booties.

"Isn't this adorable?" she asked, pointing to a red velveteen dress with gloves and booties.

"Cute," Abe said. "Get it. What do you have for the little guys' clothes?"

Nicola pulled two outfits from the cart and Abe made a face.

"What?" she asked, looking at the outfits again. "What's wrong?"

"They're too sissy looking," Abe said.

"They're red. They're Christmassy," she protested.

He shook his head. "Red velvet. Sissy. Blue or green would be better. And whatever you do, don't pick satin. You'll give the poor kid a complex."

Nicola's lips twitched. "I never would have guessed you would be opinionated about baby clothes."

"I'm not," Abe said, pulling out a blue velvet outfit

that he felt was a reasonable compromise. "I just think it's good to start out with gender appropriate clothing. No need to confuse anyone from the beginning. Half the time babies are bald, so it's already hard enough to tell the difference. What else?"

"Receiving blankets," Nicola said.

"Male or female?" he asked.

"That can't possibly matter with blankets," she said.

"Don't argue with me. We're going to make sure that nobody mistakes our girl babies for boys and our boy babies for girls."

"Ours," Nicola echoed, giving him a strange look.

Abe nodded. "Our angel babies." The way she was looking at him made him feel twitchy on the back of his neck. They selected baby blankets. "So, we're done, right? I got the bicycles and other stuff. The service department will put the bikes together and we can pick them up in two days."

"All except books," Nicola said, shoving her cart down another lane.

"Huh? There aren't any books on the list," Abe said, following after her with another cart.

"I know, but I always like to make sure each child gets a book. Reading is so very important. I sometimes even tuck one in for the mother."

Abe felt his heart soften and slid his hand behind Nicola's neck. "I would have never guessed you'd feel so maternal for people you don't even know."

He felt her stiffen and pull slightly away.

"People are capable of all kinds of things. It's best not to pigeonhole. Here are the books." She began to make her selections.

He studied her carefully. Lord, she was acting strange. Since it was after 1 a.m., it took no time to get through the checkout. He glanced at the variety of books—animal books, touch-and-smell baby books, Harry Potter and baby and child care. "Hey, what's with the baby-care books?" he asked. "Don't you think they know how to take care of a baby if they already have them?"

"This will be a great reference if something unexpected comes up. I'll pay for mine separately," she said.

"No," Abe said, pulling out his credit card. "You did the shopping. I'll do the paying."

"I'm perfectly able to—"

"I know you are," he said. "You're perfectly able to do anything you want or need to do, but I'd like to take care of this. Okay?"

She blinked at him. "Uh, okay. Thank you."

"You're welcome," he said, and they bundled up the bags and walked to his car. Her silence bothered him. He loaded the bags into his trunk, opened the passenger door to help her in then got in on his side. He closed the door behind him and looked at her. "What in hell is going on with you?"

She bit her lip. "What do you mean?"

"I mean when you got all bent out of shape when I complimented you on how maternal you were being."

She lifted one shoulder in a semishrug. "It didn't feel like a compliment. I know I've been wrapped up in my career, but there's more to me than that." She paused. "I'm not just career-girl Barbie."

"I didn't think you were," Abe said.

"Well, it sounded like it," she said, crossing her arms over her chest.

He shook his head. "Nic, I'm having a hard time following you lately. You tell me you think we should keep our relationship professional, but you admit you have feelings for me. You tell me you're not interested in marriage then get upset when I make a comment about your maternal urges. Help me out here."

She took a deep breath and nodded her head up at the sky and gave a half smile. "There's a full moon. Maybe it's bringing out the witch in me."

It had to be her hormones, Nicola thought as she entered the town house with Abe hauling in bags of toys and clothes and books. One minute, she wanted to hiss at Abe for making an idle comment on her maternal leanings. The next minute, when she saw his big hands holding blue baby booties, she wanted to hug him.

Nicola mentally rolled her eyes at herself. "Thanks for bringing them in. I can handle it from here. I just separate them based on the list and take them to the Angel Tree drop-off and we're done. Thanks so much."

Abe frowned. "I'm not letting you carry all these bags by yourself. We can divide the gifts now and take them in two days when I pick up the bicycles." He opened the bags. "I have pink baby blankets here."

"That would be Carmelita," she said.

"Tonka truck, make that two Tonka trucks," he said.

She thumbed through the lists. "Will and Eli."

And so it went until Abe had emptied all the bags and arranged the gifts in twelve piles. "You have an extra baby-care book," he said.

"We can give that to Carmelita's mother," she said quickly and made a mental note to put it in her nightstand.

Abe stood and grinned. "Looks like Santa has been here."

Her heart tripped over itself. "I guess he has. No white beard or fat belly on this Santa, though." She couldn't resist the urge to kiss him, so she did. Lifting on tiptoe, she pressed her mouth against his. The brief kiss she had planned suddenly turned into something longer, hotter and more wicked.

"What was that for?" he asked when she pulled back slightly.

"Must've been the shopping," she said, kissing him again, sliding her tongue over his when she thought about him and his crazy opinions about what kinds of clothes babies should wear. It shouldn't turn her on, but it did.

"Let me get this straight," he murmured against her mouth. "You're turned on by a midnight shopping trip to Wal-Mart?"

She slid her hands under his cashmere sweater. "I know. Sounds crazy, doesn't it? Better run while you can."

"No way," he said, tightening his arms around her. "Can't say I understand it. Tiffany's, I could get that, but Wal-Mart?"

She laughed against his throat. "It wasn't Wal-Mart. It was how generous you were, and the fact that you got into it, even with your silly opinions about the color of receiving blankets."

"They're not silly," he said then groaned. "Lord, your breasts feel good." He took her mouth and gave her a lengthy, thorough kiss that made her head spin. "Tell me you're not too tired."

"I'm not," she said. "I took a three-hour nap this afternoon."

She was being shameless, but heaven help her, she couldn't remember feeling this turned on, and it wasn't as if she could get pregnant. Already done that. Nicola had used up all her energy for denying her feelings for Abe. At least until he left for D.C. The lure of uninhibited, unprotected sex with Abe was too much.

She dropped her hands to the belt on his slacks and undid it. She unfastened buttons and slid her hands inside his briefs to cup him in her hands. Huge and hard, he let out a long hiss at her touch.

"You're moving fast, sweetheart. If you keep touching me like that, I'll be inside you in no time."

"Promise?" she said, and watched his eyes light with fire.

His mouth fastened to hers, he eased her down on the floor and pulled her sweater over her head. She tugged his over his head. He undid her bra with disconcerting speed.

"You do that very fast," she said breathlessly.

"Does it bother you?" he asked.

"I'm not sure I like thinking about how much experience it required to develop that speed."

Abe laughed and dipped his mouth over her nipple. "When I was a teenager, I swiped a bra from the laundry and practiced on my desk chair."

She smiled at the image. "Okay, that doesn't bother me as much."

"But I want to bother you, Nic." He slid his hands down to the top of her jeans and unfastened them. "I want to bother you as much as you bother me."

He dipped his mouth again to her nipple and drew it into his mouth while he unzipped her zipper and skimmed his fingers beneath the edge of her panties to the part of her that was already swollen.

Her heart hammering, her body blazing from the inside out, she shimmied to push down her jeans. "I think it's safe to say you bother me."

He stroked her and stroked her until she didn't think she

could stand it anymore. She tugged his slacks down and pulled at his tight buttocks. "Inside. I want you in—"

"Let me get a condom, babe," he said.

"You don't need one," she said breathless and impatient for him.

He gave a second look. "You're on something?"

She swallowed a knot of guilt. "I've been to the doctor."

One second later, he thrust inside her and they both sighed with pleasure.

"You feel so good," she said, wiggling beneath him. "I want more. Do me more."

Abe made a sound halfway between a prayer and a curse and began to pump inside her.

She stretched and undulated in rhythm with him, loving the way he felt inside her, rubbing her intimately, filling her. She loved the way his hard body felt over hers. He was the father of her baby. He was the sexiest man in the world to her, and for this moment he was hers, all hers.

Eight

The next morning, Nicola practically had to shove Abe out the door. Pulling her against him, he dropped kisses onto the side of her neck. "We had a late night. It's early. Let me take you back to bed."

Nicola felt a rush of arousal at how thoroughly Abe had made love to her the night before. Biting back a groan, she pulled away. "You need to leave. It's not good for your car to be parked in my driveway all night into morning. You never know when the press is watching."

"The election's over," he said, reaching for her again.

Nicola stepped aside. "You won, so they're still watching. You've fascinated them. They'll be insatiable now," she said, reaching up to touch the hard line of his chin.

"I think I'd rather make you insatiable," he said, his gaze sexually possessive.

Oh, you do, she thought. "Stop plying me with your charms. Not fair. You're forcing me to be the sensible one."

"Okay, let's be sensible," he said. "Let's go away for the weekend. Just you and me."

Nicola's heart jumped and she gasped. "Oh, that's sensible," she said in mocking agreement. "And were you planning to register under the name John Smith?" She shook her head. "What is with you? All of a sudden, you're throwing caution to the wind." She bit her lip and wandered away from him. "You're not acting very senatorial," she said in a light voice.

She felt him step behind her and loop his arms around her waist. "I told you. I want a relationship with you, Nic. I'll do anything to keep you."

Including marrying me and helping to raise our child? She swallowed the lump in her throat. "Maybe it's because you're getting ready to make a lot of changes. Going from private life to public life and moving to Washington, D.C. won't be easy."

He sighed. "I don't know what it's going to take to convince you that I want you, but I'll do it, Nic. You'll see."

Her chest tightened with a combination of stupid hope and inevitable disappointment. She felt as if she was free-falling with no parachute. She closed her eyes and reined in her emotions. It was dirty, but she was desperate. "Number one on the list of convincing me is for you to scoot back to your mansion right now," she said, stepping away from him.

He looked at her and shook his head then slid his finger over her nose. "I don't know why you're running, sweetheart, but I'm gonna catch you."

On Wednesday afternoon, Abe insisted on joining her to deliver the Angel Tree gifts. Nicola had labeled and bagged them. After they picked up the bikes, they went to the drop-off station at the mall.

Abe allowed Nicola to carry a light bag while he carried two bicycles.

"I warned you it would be crowded," Nicola said. "You'll be lucky if you don't get out of here without getting half a dozen requests for photos."

Abe laughed. "I'm in jeans, a sweater and I even put on a cap. No one will look twice."

Nicola shook her head. "For such a shrewd man, you're incredibly naive."

"What do you mean?"

"I mean people are going to look at you regardless of what you're wearing. You're one of those men who capture the attention of both men and women. Men, because they can sense you're powerful. Women, because, well…" Her gaze fell over him meaningfully. "That's obvious."

He leaned closer to her. "I love it when you look at

me like that. It makes me think I have a shot at getting you under my spell despite the fact that I'm almost twenty—"

Nicola dropped her bag and covered her ears. "If you say that one more time, I'm going to scream."

He stopped and lifted a dark eyebrow.

Another woman would have been intimidated. Nicola refused to be. "I think we can safely say we have put the age issue to bed," she said in a low voice.

His gaze dipped approvingly over her. "I think going to bed more frequently would solidify your case."

She bit her lip and tried not to smile. She absolutely shouldn't encourage him. Lord forgive her, but she couldn't resist. "From my observation, going to bed solidifies a lot more than my *case*."

"Agreed," he said with a wolfish grin. "All the more reason to go to bed."

Nicola felt the stares of curious onlookers and cleared her throat. "People are looking. We need to move."

They deposited the first gifts to the Angel Tree station, which was situated across from Santa Claus, and returned to the car to bring more. Abe finagled a cart from an employee at a department store and brought the rest of the gifts. The huge pile of gifts was attention getting. Nicola glanced around at the people staring at the gifts and Abe. "One, two, three—"

"Isn't that Abraham Danforth, our new state senator?" someone from the Santa line said.

"Bingo," Nicola said and smiled at Abe.

He shot her a look of chagrin and waved at the person who'd called his name. "Thanks and merry Christmas to you," he said.

"Hey, Senator Danforth, I voted for you. Would you mind giving me an autograph?" said a man in the Santa line with twins.

"Of course," Abe said graciously.

Nicola felt a shot of admiration. They would end up being at the mall for hours. She knew it wouldn't end with one autograph and handshake. Abe responded to the requests, kissing babies. Soon there was a line of people wanting to have their baby's pictures taken with Abe.

Transfixed, she watched him hold the assortment of squirmy, crying, sleeping, slobbering, sneezing infants with ease. Despite the fact that he had said he hadn't spent much time with his children as infants, he sure seemed to know how to handle them.

She saw him comfort a little boy, holding the baby securely and rocking from one foot to the other. Her heart twisted. She wondered if he would hold their baby. She wondered if he could grow to love and want their child instead of seeing it as a burden. She wondered if the baby would have Abe's hair or killer eyes. Her eyes turned damp.

Blinking in surprise, she turned away and swiped at her cheeks. She took a deep breath and exhaled. *Get a grip.*

"Nicola," Abe called. "What time is my meeting this afternoon?"

She glanced at her watch. "Four-thirty. I'm sorry I let it slip. We'd better get moving." Welcoming the opportunity to put on her PR hat, she stepped forward. "Senator Danforth has a telephone meeting with the majority leader this afternoon. I know he would love to stay, but I hope you'll excuse him."

"Thanks," Abe said and joined her to walk out of the mall. "Is this when I say you were right?"

"I told you that you underestimated your appeal," she said. "Even the babies liked you."

"I'll tell you my secret," he said, looping his arm around her. "It's easy to hold a baby when you know it's just for a couple of minutes and you'll be giving it right back to Mom and Dad."

And a little piece of Nicola's heart broke.

Greeting friends and family in the grand foyer of Crofthaven for the annual Christmas party, he stood beside his brother, Harold, and kept glancing in the doorway. He wondered if Nicola had skipped the greeting line and had come in the back way. He wouldn't put it past her. The staff loved her. She was probably tucked away in the kitchen conducting a taste testing and sipping some wine. Or not with the wine, he thought. He'd noticed she'd turned into a teetotaler lately. He'd also noticed that she'd been alternately passionate and aloof. Swearing under his breath, he wondered what the hell was going on with her. Every time she backed away, it made him break into a cold sweat. He didn't want to lose her.

Harold nudged him. "Let's take a break. My hand's getting tired."

Abe met his brother's gaze and felt an easing inside him. His brother was one person he'd been able to count on through thick and thin. "Won't Miranda get upset?" he asked, speaking of Harold's longtime wife.

Harold shook his head. "She won't mind. I'll tell her we'll make the rounds through the rooms. Let me get you a drink. You look like you could use it."

"Thanks, Harold," Abe said dryly, but followed his brother down the hall to Abe's private study. Abe shut the door behind him and Harold pulled out the Scotch.

"So what's the problem? Nicola?" Harold asked as he handed Abe his shot glass full of Scotch.

Abe tossed back the Scotch and felt the alcohol burn all the way down. "Is there anyone who doesn't know?"

"Maybe the press," Harold said. "But that could change in a New York minute."

"I don't think I give a damn if the press finds out," Abe said, feeling his frustration burn and rumble like acid indigestion.

Harold raised his eyebrows. "Hmm. You want to marry her?"

Abe felt years of reluctance drag at him. "I don't know about marriage. I didn't put in a stellar performance as husband the first time. You know, Harold, that I've always envied the relationship you and Miranda share."

Harold smiled and grabbed a handful of peanuts from a dish on the desk. "I got lucky. My wife's a saint and it's okay with her that I don't want to conquer the world. It was easy to let you be the Type-A son."

"The Type-A son sure screwed up the personal side of things."

Harold shrugged. "You did the best you could. Your kids are healthy, educated and successful. They can all pay for therapy if they want."

Abe chuckled and sighed. He patted his brother on the shoulder. "I couldn't have a better brother."

"Then maybe you'll take some advice from me for a change," Harold said. "You were young the first time you got married. I can tell you still have plenty of that Type-A in you, but I can also tell the professional side of things isn't popping your cork as much as it used to. You're older now, hopefully wiser. Maybe you're finally ready to put a priority on being there for somebody else."

Silent for a long moment, Abe met his brother's gaze. "When did you get so damn smart?"

Harold cracked a smile. "When you were out conquering the world."

Food was Nicola's friend again. In the parlor, she tasted strawberries dusted with powdered sugar, mini-pecan tarts, sausage balls. Her queasiness had been absent for three days in a row and she was ready to enjoy the spread at the Danforth party.

"Your stomach must be better," Abe said from behind her, causing her heart to flutter. She wondered how he managed to combine humor and sexiness in his voice.

"Much," she said, turning around to face him.

He reached past her for a strawberry and his body rubbed against hers. "Good," he said, meeting her gaze. "But I know something that's better."

He meant *her,* of course, and she felt her heart flutter again.

"I figured you came in the back door," he said.

"I wanted you to bask in your senatorial splendor with your friends and guests," she said, tongue in cheek.

He rolled his eyes. "You're full of bull and you know it. You knew I'd draft you into the receiving line."

"Which wouldn't have been at all appropriate," she pointed out, discreetly licking the tip of her finger. "Since I'm not family. I'm officially an employee, the staff, the help."

With a look of challenge in his eyes, he caught her hand and lifted it to his mouth, his tongue sliding over the finger she'd just licked. "I'm changing that."

Gasping, Nicola jerked her hand away from his and glanced around to see if anyone had seen. "Are you nuts?" she whispered.

He paused for a moment then nodded. "Yes," he said. "I am."

She fought the slow dragging sensation of seduction in her belly. He was getting dangerous. Well, he'd always been dangerous for her. But he was pulling out the stops, Lord help her. She cleared her throat. "I should go say hello to—"

"I have something I want to show you before you run away, Chicken Little," he said, taking her elbow and guiding her to the opposite corner of the room.

His accusation ruffled. "I'm not Chicken Little. I'm just being sensible while you're being totally…" She couldn't think of just one word that adequately expressed her feelings.

"Totally what?" he prompted.

Totally wonderful, irresistible, impossible. There, that was a good one. "Impossible."

He nodded and pointed toward a table. "I had the cook make this in your honor."

Nicola glanced down and saw a sheet cake that suspiciously resembled her favorite cake. Her heart melted. "Is it really Mississippi Mud Cake?"

He nodded. "There's another in the kitchen for you to take home."

Her eyes widened. "Oh, I can't eat the entire thing myself," she protested. "But maybe I could freeze part of it." She met Abe's gaze. "This was too nice. Very thoughtful." She felt a ridiculous lump of emotion form in her throat. "I don't know what to say."

"Let me deliver the other cake to you tonight after the party."

"You're not talking about just cake," she accused, but knew her voice held no punch.

"Are you complaining?" he asked, with justifiable confidence, and she knew she had been the one to justify his confidence.

Nicola chose not to respond. "I want to say hello to Harold and Miranda," she murmured and stepped backward.

He nodded with a grin, clearly knowing she was running. "I'll catch you later."

That was what she was afraid of.

Four hours later when Nicola thought she'd successfully escaped the party without Abe catching her, she lay in bed ready to put aside the book on pregnancy she'd been reading.

Her doorbell rang, and her pulse picked up. She swore under her breath because she knew who it was. Maybe if she pretended to be asleep.

The doorbell sounded again.

Three times, she told herself, clenching her eyes closed. If she could last through three rings, he would go home, she told herself. It was after midnight and he wouldn't wake her neighbors.

The doorbell sounded again and she counted to ten.

She let out a breath of air and heard pounding on her door. Her eyes flew open and she jumped out of bed, grabbing her robe. This was ridiculous.

Stomping downstairs, ready to read him the riot act, Nicola barely glanced through the peephole before she jerked open the door.

Still dressed in a dark suit that made him look lean and yummy, he stood on her front porch holding a pan in one hand and a wrapped package in the other.

She crossed her arms over her chest. "Have you looked at the time? It's after midnight."

"Good morning," he said with a nod. "May I come in?"

She wanted to say *no,* but she didn't trust him to be quiet and at least one of them had to protect his image. As soon as she closed the door behind her, she rounded on him. "Abe, I've worked very hard for the last year to help you project a dependable, mature persona to the media and the public and I don't want you sending that message down the tubes just because you've won the election."

"I think you don't understand, Nic. I'll allow my constituents to know the truth about me, but I won't change who I am for my constituents."

Frustration raced through her. This same, solid, this-is-who-I-am-love-me-or-hate-me attitude had won the election for him. She watched him set the package on the sofa table. "But you can still be discreet," she insisted.

"I'm being plenty discreet," he said, loosening his tie. "Where do you want me to put the cake?"

"In the kitchen," she said, leading the way to the small galley kitchen. She put the cake pan on the counter and turned to face him, finding herself boxed in.

She swallowed at the determined expression on his face. "I meant what I said about you being discreet."

"I meant what I said, too," he said.

"It's not discreet for your car to be in my driveway all hours of the night," she said.

"Then come back to Crofthaven."

Nicola groaned. "You're avoiding the truth."

He shook his head and gently backed her against the wall. "No, sweetheart. You are." He lowered his head and took her mouth in a sensual, possessive kiss that made her knees lose their starch.

He pulled back and she could feel the reluctance emanating from him. "Open the gift after I've left. I'll pick you up tomorrow night at seven."

Catching her breath, she blinked at him. "What's tomorrow night at seven?"

"Cocktail party at the Robert Billings house."

"That's not business."

"He was my biggest campaign donor. That makes it business. Don't worry. It's semiformal. I'm sure you have something. I'd like to stay, but I've decided to wait for an invitation."

She stared at him for a long moment. She felt as if she was suffering from whiplash. He'd been pushing her so hard. And what was with the gift and the cake?

He rubbed his thumb over her bottom lip. "You need to admit your feelings for me before we can make progress."

Progress? What kind of progress? He slid his finger inside her mouth. She instinctively cupped her tongue around his finger.

He shot her a look of sexual approval. "That's what your body does when I slide inside you. You close around me like you can't get enough of me. It's okay, Nic, because I can't get enough of you, either. You just need to say it aloud, and then we can move on."

She closed her teeth around his finger and watched his eyes widen in surprise. Chuckling, he shook his head and brushed his mouth over her cheek. "Remember how I taste when you go to sleep tonight. Remember how I feel inside you when you close your eyes. All it will take is one word," he whispered. "Stay." He nuzzled her ear and turned away.

She noticed he didn't appear to have any difficulty walking. His knees were just fine. She, however, was still propping herself against the kitchen counter.

He would wait a very long time, like forever, before he got an invitation from her, she promised herself as she watched him leave the town house. She would put a sock in her mouth before she would invite him to stay overnight.

Nine

She needed to be more firm with Abe.

She needed to be more firm with herself.

As she stomped around her town house getting ready for a cocktail party she technically shouldn't be required to attend with a man she definitely shouldn't be spending so much time with, Nicola muttered early New Year's resolutions under her breath.

"No more slipping into a sexual stupor when he kisses me," she told herself as she stepped into black pumps.

"No more kissing," she added, walking toward the den.

"And no more accepting gifts," she said, shooting the evil eye at the still wrapped gift he'd left her the night before. Abe Danforth was wealthy. He could afford the kinds of gifts most women would find irresistible, such as fine jewelry, designer clothing and hot little sport cars.

But Nicola refused to weaken on this matter. It would make her feel sleazy if he gave her extravagant gifts. Damn shame she had such principles because she wouldn't mind a new car, and even though she wasn't a jewelry person, she'd always secretly wanted some killer diamond stud earrings and one diamond ring large enough that it would require a crane to lift it. She'd never revealed her licentious wishes to anyone.

Even though she knew her relationship with Abe was—*had been,* she corrected herself mentally. *Past tense.* Even though she knew her relationship with Abe hadn't been tawdry, she didn't like the idea of other people casting her as the trophy wife. She didn't like it for herself and she liked it even less for Abe.

So, even though she was dying of curiosity as to what was in the gift box from Abe, she wouldn't open it. Joan of Arc would be proud.

The doorbell rang and she jumped. Not a good start for a woman who was supposed to be cool, calm, in control and unseduceable. Telling her heart not to race, she slowly walked to the door and marshaled her defenses. Lord help her, she would need them.

She opened the door and there he stood with a bouquet of flowers that reminded her of peppermint candy. Red and white roses with carnations, greenery and baby's breath. It was gorgeous and just what she'd said she liked.

"I brought you some flowers. I asked the florist to make it look Christmassy. What do you think?"

"I think you shouldn't have," she said and sighed. He'd ordered the flowers himself and that made the bouquet special in itself.

"You're welcome. I've already done it," he said, walking past her toward the kitchen. "Do you know if you have something to put them in?"

"Probably not," she said, determined to remain firm even though she felt like an ingrate. She heard him rustling under the kitchen counter then the sound of running water.

"This will work," he said, returning to the den. "Where do you want them?"

"That table will be fine." She waved her hand. "Listen, Abe, I know we've discussed this before and—"

"You look beautiful," he said, coming toward her.

Panicking, Nicola lifted her fingers in the sign of the cross as if he were a vampire with special powers. "Stop."

He laughed, folding her hands in his. "What's this? I'm not out for blood."

"You've got to stop this," she said. "You've got to stop trying to wear me down. I know what's best for me and I know what's best for your image and it's best that we don't carry on in front of the world. It's best that we don't carry on period."

His face turned serious. "I'm not just carrying on, Nic."

She pulled her hands away from his and covered her eyes with them. "I wish I knew what it was going to take to convince you that—"

"You didn't open the gift."

She opened her eyes and felt a twinge of guilt over the disappointment she heard in his voice. "I don't think I should be accepting gifts from you."

"That's bull," he said. "It's not as if I'm plying you with diamonds and you're my mistress—" He broke off as if he was rethinking the notion. "Although it's not a bad idea."

She lifted her hand. "Don't even go there."

"I want you to open the gift," he said.

She crossed her arms over her chest, mentally girding her resolve. "I won't."

He made a guttural sound of exasperation. "All I want you to do is open it. You can refuse it, but only after you open it." He sat down on the couch. "I'm not going anywhere until you do. And if we show up late for the cocktail party, everyone will wonder why and I'll have to tell the truth because I'm honest Abe. I'll have to tell them that you wouldn't open the gift I got for you."

Frustration roared through her. He knew exactly how to get at her. "Okay, okay. I'll open it and then you're taking it back."

"Open it first," he said.

Wishing she didn't feel so emotional, Nicola bit her

lip as she tore the beautiful paper from the box. When she found it taped, Abe offered his pocket knife. She opened the box and saw hardcover books, several of them. She picked up the first one and read the title. *"Little Women."*

A lump formed in her throat and her eyes started to burn. She met Abe's gaze through eyes that threatened tears.

"The complete works of Louisa May Alcott. Original editions," he said quietly. "I had to do a little looking to find one of those."

When she didn't say anything, he stood and looked at her curiously. "You want to give them back to me?"

Her emotion choking her, she swallowed twice before she could speak. "You are a beast," she whispered. The books left diamond stud earrings in the dust.

The Billings home was an historic landmark, grand, but not as grand as Crofthaven. It was beautifully decorated, although a bit too Victorian for her taste. Nicola noticed that heads turned within a minute of Abe entering the front foyer. After a year of being in close contact with Abe, she should be accustomed to the electricity he generated just by walking into a room, but she wasn't.

"Abe, I'm so glad you could come," Robert Billings said, extending his hand.

"Wouldn't miss it," Abe said. "You remember Nicola, don't you?"

"How could I forget? The best mover and shaker in the South," Robert said with a smile. "Will you be going to D.C. with the new senator from Georgia?"

"N—"

"We're negotiating," Abe interjected. "Where's Gloria? She's done a great job with the house."

Robert winced. "I've already broken two of her angels. I'll be glad when Christmas is over."

"Abe Danforth, you're just the man I'm looking for," a woman called from across the foyer.

Nicola identified the woman as Gloria, Robert's wife. She had looped her arm through another woman's elbow, Vivian Smith's.

"Abe, I know you've been terribly busy with the campaign with no time for a social life, but now you can catch your breath and have some fun. You've met Vivian, haven't you?"

"Yes, I have," Abe said, extending his hand. "Vivian, I appreciate all your support. You've been very generous."

Abe gave a formal response, Nicola noticed. Vivian looked hopeful.

"Vivian, have you met Nicola Granville?" Abe asked.

"Oh, you were his campaign manager, weren't you?" Gloria interjected. "This girl is quick as a whip. Listen, we won't make you hang around us old folks tonight. I invited the new surgeon in town and I'm sure he'd love to meet you. Come along," she said.

Nicola shot Abe an I-told-you-so glance. "Very nice to meet you, Vivian. That color looks fabulous on you. I'll see you later," she said to Abe.

"Soon," he said.

Keeping track of Nicola with his peripheral vision, he was aware of every move she made. Although he'd made as much small talk as he'd wanted within two minutes, Vivian seemed determined to prolong the conversation. Nicola had no shortage of men wanting to talk to her, he noticed sourly. She lit up the room with her smile and laughter.

"She's so young and full of energy," Vivian said, looking at Nicola.

"Not that young," Abe said and caught Vivian's double take. "I mean she's not twenty-something. She's mature for her age."

"Will she be joining your staff in Washington?"

The woman's fishing irritated Abe, especially since he couldn't say, *yes, she is.* "I haven't made final arrangements for my staff."

"Do you think you'll mind the change in weather?"

Abe frowned. "What do you mean?"

"Well, it gets cold in the winter. How will you stay warm?"

Abe blinked at the coy expression on her face. Oh, no, she was offering to help him stay warm. Time's up, he told himself. He cleared his throat. "I have an excellent wool coat," he said. "Vivian, it's good seeing you again. Again, I appreciate your support. Excuse me while I get some water."

He grabbed a glass of water on his way to Nicola, who was talking with a young man. "Hello," he said with a nod to the man.

"Senator Danforth, this is Dr. Jenson. He's the new surgeon Gloria was telling us about."

Abe extended his hand. "Welcome to Savannah," he said.

"Congratulations on the election, Senator. Nicola was just telling me she won't be going to Washington, so I thought I'd check with the hospital administration about using her services."

Abe ground his teeth. "I haven't given up on bringing Nicola to Washington with me," he said. "I'll use every means at my disposal to persuade her. Excuse us for a moment," he continued, barely taking a breath as he slid his hand around Nicola's waist. "Thanks."

He led her into the hallway.

She shrugged out of his embrace and looked at him as if he'd lost his mind. "Abe, you're acting like a territorial caveman," she whispered.

"Between Gloria branding me as 'one of the old folks' and Vivian offering to keep me warm in Washington, I'm feeling a little primitive," he said.

Nicola's eyes widened. "Vivian offered to keep you warm in Washington?"

He nodded, slightly mollified by the outrage in her voice. "She went on and on about how *young* you were."

"I'm not that young," she retorted.

"That's what I told her."

She blinked then chuckled. "You can't blame her for going after you. You're handsome, intelligent, wealthy, sexy. Plus you've got that senior citizen's discount."

Abe scowled and something inside him ripped. "I've got two words for you, little girl." He glanced up at the mistletoe above their heads. "Merry Christmas," he said and took her in an open-mouth kiss.

Horrified by Abe's public display of passion, Nicola fled to the powder room. She splashed water on her face to cool her cheeks. She swore under her breath. Her entire body was hot and she couldn't say it was entirely due to anger or indignation or embarrassment. Oh, no, that man could kiss like nobody's business.

Trying to pull herself together, she struggled with her distress. Why was he making this so difficult? Was he one of those men who was attracted by the unattainable? Then as soon as he attained it, he lost interest?

Taking several deep breaths, she stepped into the hallway smack-dab into Gloria Billings. "Oh, excuse me. I'm so sorry."

"No problem," Gloria said.

Nicola felt the woman studying her face and tried to

draw the attention away from herself. "It's a lovely party. You're a terrific hostess."

"Thank you. It comes from experience," she said with a smile. She paused. "Aren't you a little young for him?"

Nicola froze. "I don't know what you're talking about."

"A little young for the senator," Gloria said in a lowered, but knowing voice. "I saw you under the mistletoe."

Her heart slammed against her rib cage. "That was really nothing."

"It didn't look like nothing to me," Gloria said with a laugh. "Listen, you're young. Abe isn't. He may seem like great sugar-daddy material, but he needs a mature woman to handle him."

Nicola dropped her jaw. Anger and amazement rushed through her. "Number one, anyone who calls Abe a sugar daddy is greatly underestimating him. Number two, I'm no immature sugar-daddy hunter. Number three, none of this matters, because Abe and I aren't planning a future together." Still infuriated, but fearing her mouth would get her in trouble, she shrugged. "Thank you for a lovely party."

Twenty minutes later, Abe and Nicola left. He turned to her in the car. "You're being ridiculous, Nicola. When are you going to talk?"

Nicola looked at him in exasperation. "I'm being ridiculous! I'm not the one who initiated a French kiss at the home of the biggest busybody in Savannah."

He waved his hand as if she was concerned for nothing. "What's she going to do? Put on a billboard that Abe Danforth kissed Nicola Granville? So what? I'm not married. Neither are you."

"There's more than you to consider," she said, thinking of the baby. The more attention Abe drew to their relationship, the more attention there would be drawn to their child.

"What do you mean by that?"

Nicola bit her lip. "I mean, this doesn't make me look good. The man often comes out on top in these situations when people start gossiping. If this gets out, the next person who hires me will wonder if I sleep with all my clients."

Abe looked appalled. For all of one moment. "I can solve that. You can work for me."

Nicola sighed. "I don't want to work for you. I feel like a broken record."

"Then play a new song," he suggested, pulling into her driveway. "I guess this means you won't be inviting me in," he said.

"That's correct," she said crisply and opened her car door.

He caught her arm in a firm, but gentle grasp. "Nicola?"

She took a deep breath and glanced around. "What?"

"I've never felt this way about a woman before."

Her heart stopped. "I have to go," she said. "I'll talk to you later." She scrambled out of the car and up the steps to her front door as if the hounds of hell were after her. She wondered how quickly he'd get over his feelings for her once she told him about the baby.

"Did you read the gossip column this morning?" Nicola asked Abe as he presented her with a year's supply of Skittles and walked through her front door.

Judging by the anxiety on her face, Abe figured she was going to consume all five bags this week since they were Nic's form of "nervous food." "I hate to show my age in this area, but I don't read the gossip column very often," Abe said. "I'm more likely to read the *Financial Times*."

Nicola dogged his steps to her den. "Their gossip columnist writes blind items. She describes the people so that readers know who is being discussed. This morning, it said, "Hot from holiday-party central, a certain newly elected representative was caught kissing his much younger campaign director under the mistletoe."

Nicola dumped all the two-pound bags of Skittles on the table except one and ripped it open. "I warned you this would happen."

Abe shrugged. "If they didn't name names, then what's the harm? Elections were held in November. Technically, everyone is newly elected."

"But you know it won't stop there," she said. "It's bound to show up in some other newspaper or magazine or on a radio show."

He watched her put three of the candies into her mouth. "So the worst thing that could happen is you'd have to make an honest man of me and marry me," he said, but knew he was only half joking.

"Oh, don't be ridiculous."

Ouch.

She chewed and swallowed. "I already told you I don't want to have the reputation that I get involved with my clients."

The situation seemed simple to Abe. "The truth is you don't get involved with your clients, but you have gotten involved with one. One who is single just like you."

She bit her lip, looking terrified.

He shook his head and tugged at her mouth. "Stop abusing your lip. I don't understand why you're so upset about this unless you're ashamed of your relationship with me."

Her jaw worked and she moved her head in a circle. She stepped back. "I'm not ashamed of our relationship. It's just not a real relationship."

"What the hell do you mean by that?"

She paced around the den. "I mean, look at the way it all started. Late one night, we got carried away. Then we told each other we should stop. And we did, sorta," she said with a wince. "We didn't start out choosing to get involved romantically. We just fell into it. I don't think that's the way a real, solid relationship starts."

Something in her tone made his gut twist. Abe absently rubbed at his stomach. "A relationship is like a journey. Just because it starts on one road doesn't mean it stays on that road."

"Yes, but don't you think we got involved because of the passion of the campaign? The passion and intensity of everything that was going on?" she asked, popping three more Skittles.

"That may have contributed, but that's not the only reason. It's not the major reason." His gut tightened another notch. "The major reason for me is that I've never felt a connection with a woman like I have with you. You don't agree with me just because my last name is Danforth. I feel like I'm on equal footing with you."

He saw a half-dozen emotions cross her face so quickly he couldn't identify them all, but he did see raw want and need and despair. He didn't understand the despair.

"I trust you, Nic. After all we've been through, I think you can handle me." Unaccustomed to exposing himself this way, he paused and chuckled. "That probably sounds arrogant as hell."

Her lips twitched. "No. It's actually a compliment." Her smile fell. "But you don't know everything about me and I'm just not sure—" Her voice broke off and she bit her lip again.

Realization dawned and he felt as if she'd stabbed him. "You're not sure of me," he said. "You don't trust me."

"Of course I trust you," she countered. "I wouldn't have been effective as your campaign manager if I didn't trust you and I wouldn't have gone to bed with you if I hadn't trusted you on some level."

"But you're not sure you can trust me in a real relationship," he said. "I was good for a secret affair, and a hot roll in the sack, but not for anything you call real." He shook his head. This was his worst fear realized, that he was incapable of having an intimate relationship with another human being. Nic had told him just as much and he was left with the worst emptiness he'd ever experienced in his life.

Ten

Nicola didn't hear from Abe for three days. Every hour that passed, she felt the distance between them grow exponentially. She hated hurting Abe and she knew she'd hurt him, but she also knew he didn't want any more children.

Nicola couldn't bear the thought of bringing up her child in a home where the father gave grudging attention and affection. She still hid scars of her father's abandonment. Add to that, the thought of watching Abe's feelings for her die a slow death because he didn't want the child. Nicola couldn't stand it. Better to nip things between them now before they went any further.

She told herself to be strong, but every other moment

she doubted herself. What if Abe could accept their baby? What if he felt the same joy she did about having a child?

What if she won the lottery?

Nicola focused on the baby, devouring books on baby and child care, pregnancy and labor and delivery. She played Mozart music every night despite the fact that it was entirely too early to have any effect on the baby. When she visited department stores, she lingered in the infant department, wondering if her baby would be a girl or boy. It was way, way too early, but she bought a beautiful leather baby album for recording everything from the baby's first burp to the baby's first steps.

She might be facing parenthood alone, but she was going to do her best, her absolute best for this child. It was tough, but she also began to discreetly investigate job possibilities in California. She hated the idea of leaving Savannah. So much had happened to her here during the last year.

The fourth night after she'd last seen Abe, and yes, she was counting, the phone woke her. She groped for the phone, glancing at the clock. One o'clock in the morning.

"Hello, Nicola? This is Lea."

Nicola sat up in bed, her heart racing. Lea was the illegitimate daughter Abe had fathered during a special mission in Vietnam. Abe hadn't even known of her existence until this year, and it had been quite an ordeal, but a relationship between them had begun to grow.

"I'm here," Nicola said. "What is it, Lea?"

"I'm at the hospital. Harold, Michael and Reid are here, too. Something's wrong with Abe."

Nicola's blood ran cold.

"What's wrong? What is it? Was he in an accident?"

"No accident," Lea said. "He developed terrible chest pain. Harold had to force him to go to the emergency room. He's being evaluated right now. I—I thought you would want to know."

"Which hospital?" Nicola asked, throwing off her covers.

Lea told her and Nicola hung up. Her heart beating a mile a minute, she stripped off her nightgown and blindly reached for a sweater and slacks.

There's something wrong with Abe.

Her hands shook as she pulled the zipper up on her slacks.

There's something wrong with Abe.

A sob escaped her throat. He couldn't die. What if she lost him? What if her baby never met his father? Unable to do anything with her hair, she pulled it up in a loose bun, yanked on some socks, stepped into shoes and grabbed a cloak.

She was so rattled she had to return to the house for her purse. Jamming the keys into the ignition of her car, she started toward the hospital with a thousand prayers on her lips.

Bursting through the E.R. doors, Nicola immediately

spotted Harold, Lea, Michael and Abe's son Reid. "How is he?" she asked. "Have you heard anything yet?"

Harold shook his head. "Sorry." He reached for her and embraced her. "The good news is he was conscious when we brought him in and giving me hell for making him come to the E.R."

Nicola nodded, feeling a sliver of relief, but still anxious. "How did you know? How did it happen?"

"I found him in the kitchen. He was doubled over clutching his chest. Scared the daylights out of me." Harold ran a nervous hand over his thinning hair. "You know he's strong as an ox. Nothing gets to him. He can run on less sleep and less food than us normal mortals. He's got more energy than men half his age. I just take for granted that he's going to be Superman forever, but you know even Superman had to deal with kryptonite."

Nicola felt her panic return. *Abe doubled over, clutching his chest.* The image of it stopped her heart. She swallowed over her dry throat. "How long has he—"

"We've been here a little over an hour. If we don't hear something soon, I'll talk to the nurse."

Nicola wanted to talk to the nurse now. She wanted to go to Abe and make sure he was okay.

Harold took her hands. "You're as pale as a ghost and your hands are cold as ice. Abe hasn't said anything the last few days, but I can tell something's bothering him. Do you have any ideas?"

Guilt suffused her. "We talked the other day and it

ended badly. I haven't talked with him since." Her eyes burned and her throat closed up. She fought tears, but they overflowed. "He can't die, Harold," she whispered. "He can't die."

"I'm going to kill my brother," Abe said to the attending physician.

"Your brother may have saved your life, Mr. Danforth. A bleeding ulcer can kill. As long as you take your medication regularly and watch your diet, then you'll be fine."

"Okay, so I can get out of this blasted nightgown and go home now?"

The doctor nodded. "Would you like me to talk to your family?"

"No. I want to see their faces when I tell them I'm finally getting ulcers instead of just giving them," Abe said.

Pulling on his clothes, he slid his feet into his shoes. He thought of Nicola and his gut hurt again. Hard to believe, but a woman had given him an ulcer. He'd better get used to that gnawing, empty feeling. She may as well have given him the big heave-ho the other night. Jamming his prescription into his pocket, he walked to the emergency waiting room. Four heads popped in his direction. His brother, Harold, Lea and Michael, and his son Reid.

"Dad?"

"Abe?" his brother said in disbelief. "If you tell me they let you walk away from a coronary, then I'll eat my hat."

"No heart attack," Abe said. "I have an ulcer."

At that moment he saw Nicola step from behind Harold and his heart jumped.

Harold shook his head. "*You* have an ulcer, but we've always said you're the one who gives the ulcers."

Abe didn't waver from looking into Nicola's eyes. She looked both frightened and relieved, confused and something more. Something deeper that gave him hope. She looked as if his little visit to the E.R. had scared her to death. "Yeah, well it looks like someone else has been giving me ulcers."

He bullied Nicola into returning to Crofthaven with him. He knew she wouldn't cave to his every demand for long, so he decided he would maximize her moment of weakness. It wasn't nice, but being without Nicola made him feel a lot less than not nice. Being without Nicola made him feel as if he lived in a vacuum.

He ran into resistance pretty quickly in the foyer. She hadn't taken her eyes off of him since they'd walked into Crofthaven. It was as if she was assuring herself that he truly was okay.

Which she seemed to have accomplished when he told her he wanted her to stay the night in his bed.

"I'm not sleeping with you," she said for the second time.

"Why not? You have a medicinal effect on me."

She shook her head, clearly still rattled. "You need your rest."

"I'll rest better with you in my bed," he said, pulling her into his arms.

"Only you," she muttered into his chest.

"What *only me?*" he asked.

"Only you would go to the E.R. and want to have sex the same night," she said in an exhausted voice.

Abe took in her wan face and switched gears. "We don't have to have sex. I just want you beside me."

"I have a hard time believing that," she said.

"You don't trust me, huh?"

She opened her mouth then closed it. "I'm just speaking from experience. I've never shared a bed with you when we didn't make love."

Granted, it would be tough. He would have to be on his deathbed not to want to make love to Nicola. But maybe this was part of his proving ground. "Maybe you should see if I'm good for my word," he said, laying down the challenge, knowing she had a tough time turning down a challenge from him.

She covered her eyes and groaned. "Okay, okay. I'll stay with you tonight. If you try to make love to me, then I will have proved my point."

There would be no *trying,* Abe thought. There would only be doing. But not tonight. "And if I don't?"

"Then we'll see," she said evasively. "Can I borrow one of your shirts for the night?"

* * *

When Nicola awakened the next morning, she felt Abe watching her before she opened her eyes. "You're supposed to be resting."

Propped on his elbow, he slid his fingers through her hair. "I'm enjoying the view."

She smiled, closing her eyes again as she luxuriated in him stroking her hair. "You're so kind. I'm sure I look like a train wreck. You scared me to death last night."

"Fair is fair."

She opened her eyes and stared at him, but still didn't move away from his touch. "What do you mean by that?"

"You give me an ulcer. I scare you to death. Fair is fair," he said, continuing to run his fingers gently over her hair.

His touch had a drugging effect on her. It was hard to sustain the urge to slap him when she had an equal urge to purr. Nicola forced herself to move. "If I'm the cause of your ulcer, then I definitely should leave."

"Whoa, whoa," Abe said, blocking her with his arm. "I meant your leaving causes my ulcer."

She met his gaze and felt a melting sensation at his confession. "You're sure about that?"

He nodded. "Sure."

She closed her eyes. "Okay, then you can stroke my hair again."

He chuckled. "I never knew how much you liked this until you told me your mother used to do it."

"It's so soothing," she said. "It almost has a hypnotic effect on me."

"Ah," he said. "A secret power. I'll have to use it wisely."

She smiled. "I said almost. Besides, you already have enough secret powers."

"Is that so?" he asked.

"Yes, it is," she said, opening her eyes and looking into his. Her heart welled with love. Oh, damn, this was inconvenient.

"Nicola, seeing you in my bed when I wake up is the most beautiful thing in the world."

"Now I know you must need glasses because I know how I looked last night. I was a mess inside and out and—"

"Hush," he said, covering her mouth with his finger. "I'm the authority on what I believe is beautiful. Have dinner with me tonight."

Her heart tripped. After last night, she couldn't find it in her to say no. Her mind kept playing the scene in the emergency room over and over. What if they had lost him? "Where?"

"Wherever you want."

"My place. I'll fix."

"Still too chicken to be seen with me in public?" he asked, rubbing her lip with his index finger.

"I prefer the term prudent."

"I don't want to be just your secret lover," he told her.

She swallowed over a lump in her throat. "You could never be just my secret lover."

He lowered his mouth to hers and kissed her. It was an easy, take-your-time kind of kiss that still managed to make her dizzy.

He pulled back and sighed. His eyes reminded her of a wild lion, possessive and predatory. "I want to make love to you," he said. "I won't because I promised I wouldn't. I just want you to know that my morning shower is going to be cold and it's all your fault."

Okay, so she cheated. Although for the most part, her nausea had passed, Nicola still couldn't face the sight of raw meat, and since Abe was definitely a carnivore kind of man, she ordered takeout from one of her favorite seafood restaurants. Three portions of shrimp fettuccini just in case he wanted seconds.

So, how did she tell him she was pregnant? And when? More than ever, Nicola knew she had to tell him. But did it have to be tonight? Couldn't she have just one more evening of Abe and his delicious attention without sharing the knowledge of the baby?

Heaven help her, she was greedy. She felt guilty and frustrated. She wished the news would thrill him, but he'd made it clear it wouldn't. It was going to change everything.

As she heated bread sticks and prepared salad, she brainstormed how to tell him. She was a PR person. If there was a perfect way to communicate the news, then she should know how to do it.

"Guess what? You're going to be a father. Again." She practiced and cringed.

"I'm pregnant," she said. That didn't sound right, either.

"You're still a stud and you have Olympic swimmers. I can prove it."

"I don't expect you to marry me. I'll raise the baby on my own," she whispered. That felt closest to the truth, but she didn't know if she could say it and look him in the eye at the same time.

"Okay, so maybe tonight is not the night to tell him," she said, but knew she needed to give herself a deadline. It seemed cruel to tell him before Christmas. That would definitely blow the holiday for him. She felt a twist at the knowledge. Oh, how she wished things could be different. In a different circumstance, the news would be like a gift.

She bit her lip as tears burned her eyes. Nicola pressed her fingers to her eyes to keep her mascara from running. These emotional swings were hell on eye makeup.

The day after Christmas, she decided. Seven days. That way, he could enjoy the holiday, eat his meal in peace and hopefully by that time his ulcer medication would be fully into his system.

She set the dining-room table with the china provided by the owner along with water and wineglasses. She went ahead and poured water in both her water and wineglass to head off questions from Abe. Since it was just a few moments before he was to arrive, she opened the pinot noir.

The doorbell rang and she smiled to herself. Abe was always prompt. She met him at the door and felt another ounce of relief at the sight of him. "How are you?" she asked.

"Great now," he said and stepped inside. "Dinner smells good."

Nicola wrapped her arms around him and buried her face in his chest.

He slid his around her. "What's this?"

"Indulge me," she said with a sigh. "I still want to make sure you're all right."

He chuckled and the sound gently rumbled through her. "I'll indulge you anytime, Nic."

She tugged him toward the table. "Come on. I have dinner ready for you. Shrimp fettuccini."

His eyes widened. "I'm impressed. I didn't know you could cook. This looks on par with Julian's Seafood Parlor," he raved.

There was a reason it looked on par with Julian's, because that was where she'd gotten it. And maybe she'd tell him that some other time. "Thanks. I hope you enjoy it."

He held her chair and motioned for her to sit down. "Thank you again." So gentlemanly, she thought, she almost felt guilty not fessing up to the Julian's takeout.

He sat across from her and lifted his wineglass to hers in a toast. "To many future dinners," he said, then added wickedly. "And breakfasts, too."

She laughed and clicked her glass with his. It was probably a good thing that she couldn't drink wine. Abe's undivided attention was already enough to muddle her mind.

They ate for a few moments in silence. "You said something the other night that made me think," he said.

Nicola cringed. Their talk had preceded the bout with his ulcer and the terrifying trip to the E.R. "Do we have to talk about the other night?"

"Yes, but don't worry. You were partly right," he said.

"Excuse me?" She wasn't accustomed to seeing Abe make many concessions.

"I thought about what you know about me, which is everything. The nature of running for political office means you have to reveal everything, warts and all. And you're a fool if you don't let your campaign director know everything in advance because she can't prepare."

She savored a bite of the shrimp fettuccini and nodded. "True."

"You know everything about me, but I only know what was on your résumé and what little bit I've been able to glean besides that."

She shrugged. "The election wasn't about me. It was about you."

"Yes, but the election's over, Nic. And our relationship is about us, not just me. I realized I don't even know your five-year personal plan."

Nicola felt a knot in her stomach. "When you interviewed me, I told you what I planned to be doing in five years. Managing the campaign for presidential candidate Abe Danforth."

"That's professional," he said, a grin playing around his hard mouth. "I want your personal five-year plan."

"I haven't given that a lot of thought. Have you? Do you know what your personal five-year plan is?"

"I didn't until this election. I know I want a better relationship with my children." He paused and met her gaze. "And I know I want you in my life."

Her heart caught at the intensity in his words. She swallowed a sip of water. "Honestly, I don't feel like I have a lot of control over what happens to me personally. I don't feel like I can say, it's December 20 and I want Mr. Right to walk through my door within three months and he will be this tall and weigh this much and love me so much he can't live without me even though I have flaws and baggage."

Abe leaned forward. "I have five children who have ambivalent feelings toward me, one of whom I didn't know existed until this year. I had an unsuccessful marriage and I was unfaithful to my wife. I live in a glass house because I've chosen to represent my state in public office. And I have an ulcer. I bet you can't top that baggage."

Nicola thought about the baby she carried. She thought about the baby she'd given up so many years ago. "That's debatable," she said.

He lifted an eyebrow and looked down for a long moment. "So were you a hooker or a terrorist before you became my campaign manager?"

Eleven

Were you a hooker or a terrorist?

Nicola glared at Abe, but couldn't disguise a chuckle. "Neither, thank you. But I did have a personal life."

"How many lovers have you had?"

She widened her eyes. "Oh, that's pretty personal."

"I'll tell you about my lovers if you'll tell me about yours."

The dare was there in his eyes. She should turn it down, but when it came to Abe, she had an insatiable curiosity. "Okay. How many for you?"

"Six," he said.

"Any you thought you were in love with?" she couldn't resist asking.

"Two," he said. "My wife and one other woman."

Nicola wasn't going to ask about the other woman. "Four for me, including my high school sweetheart. I thought I was in love with each of them for at least five minutes."

"Which one was your biggest heartbreak?"

"None of them. My mother dying was my biggest heartbreak," she said. It still hurt to remember how unprepared she'd been for how her life would change.

He nodded in sympathy. "It doesn't matter when you lose your parents. You still feel orphaned. And you were orphaned at a young age. So were my kids when my wife died."

She nodded. "But they had some security. And Harold."

"You didn't," he said. "I know that losing your mother was a terrible ordeal for you. It may sound crazy, but I want to try to find a way to make up for it."

Her heart expanded in her chest. "I think that's the most caring thing anyone has ever said to me. I feel the same way when I see you beating yourself up over your relationship with your children or even your late wife."

He reached for her hand. "I'm no expert on relationships, but being protective of each other, that would be a good quality, wouldn't it?"

"Yes, I think so."

"What was your second biggest heartbreak?"

"Besides not having Jon Bon Jovi propose to me when I was a teenager?"

He chuckled. "Yes."

"Probably having my high school boyfriend bail on me senior year," she said.

"Before senior prom?" he asked.

She paused then nodded. "Yeah, before prom," she said, but she was thinking about when she'd gotten pregnant. She'd never been more alone.

"And what about your other lovers?"

She shrugged. "They were temporary."

"So I don't have to kill three men?"

She smiled slowly. "No. Mentioning it is enough."

He took a drink of wine then a second almost as if he was fortifying himself. Nicola was filled with uneasy expectation.

"Do you know why I want to be with you?"

She shook her head. A few smart-mouth answers came to mind, but the look in his eyes quelled them.

He took another sip of wine. "Harold jokes about me being the type-A brother, the overachiever. But I'm human and I can't go ninety miles per hour all the time. I've spent the better part of my life avoiding downtime. Downtime gave me time to reflect on my failures." He cleared his throat. "In those quiet moments, I always felt completely alone. When you're with me, I don't feel lonely. I feel okay."

His confession rocked her. Abe wasn't a man for emotional disclosures and that he would trust her with his deep feelings left her speechless. She knew exactly what he was talking about. If she kept busy, then she didn't have time to think about what was really bothering her. She didn't need peace. Exhaustion took its place. Even now, he was looking at her and she knew he was waiting to see if she understood what he was describing.

She couldn't stay in her seat. The table between them might as well have been the Red Sea. Rising, she walked around the table to him and he stood. She touched his face.

He hadn't flirted or flattered. He'd just opened a door to his heart for her.

"You're such an amazing man. So amazing, I sometimes can't believe you're real."

"Oh, I'm real," he said, capturing her hand and holding it against his cheek. "I've got the ulcer medication to prove it."

She chuckled, but she felt all jittery inside, as if she was facing something momentous. She couldn't get close enough to him. She wanted to feel his heartbeat inside her. She wanted to hold him all night long, hold him so long that he would forget about feeling lonely at least for a while. She wanted to forget everything, all the problems that loomed around the corner, everything except this moment with Abe.

"I can't find my socks," she said.

He looked at her in confusion. "Socks?"

"Inside joke," she said.

"With who?"

"Me," she said and sighed. "When you told me you

would wait for me to invite you to stay with me, I told myself I would stuff a sock in my mouth before I gave you your invitation." Her heart was hammering. "I'm out of socks."

He gave a half smile, but his gaze was still watchful and waiting.

"Will you stay with me tonight?"

"Oh, yes," he said and kissed her.

Within seconds, the sweetness in his kiss turned to something sharper and edgier. He sifted his fingers through her hair. "The way you feel drives me crazy. The way you smell," he said, nuzzling her hair.

"And your body," he said, sliding his hands down her shoulders, along the sides of her breasts to her hips.

"You make me feel like I have the best body in the world and I know I don't," she said, feeling her internal temperature climb.

"You're wrong," he said, skimming his hands over her breasts again. "Your breasts are perfect. In my hands, in my mouth." He groaned, and the sound ricocheted from nerve ending to nerve ending.

He tugged her sweater upward and she lifted her hands over her head like a child. He touched her bra with gentle fingers and her breasts grew heavy and sensitive. She craved his touch. She wanted his hands on her everywhere. A crazy primitive need she couldn't explain even to herself, but she wanted every evidence of desire he could give her.

Pulling down the straps of her bra, she watched his gaze lower to her nipples. His eyes turned dark and she felt the tips of her breasts tighten. She unbuttoned his shirt and he helped then pulled her against him so that her breasts meshed with his hard chest.

Her sigh of pleasure mingled with his.

"You're like wine I'm supposed to sip, but I can't help gulping," he muttered. "And you have on way too many clothes."

The smell of his aftershave and his closeness had the same effect on her as two glasses of wine, a great buzz. She unfastened her slacks, pushed them over her hips and they slid to the floor.

He immediately slipped his hands beneath her panties to cup her bottom. "You have the best rear end known to mankind."

"And here I always thought I could serve tea on it," she said.

He laughed and squeezed her bottom, but his laugh was cut short when she lowered her hands to the fly of his pants. She wanted nothing between them, not even skin.

He took her mouth in a French kiss that left her breathless and left them both without underwear. She felt him hard against her belly as his tongue seduced hers.

She wrapped her hand around his hardness and he groaned. "I brought protection this time."

"I've already taken care of it," she said. One benefit

of pregnancy, she said to herself and let out a breathless chuckle.

He slid his hand between her legs and gave a moan of approval. "You're wet and so warm. You feel so good, so—"

He broke off when she slid to her knees and kissed his belly. "Oh, Nic, you—"

She took him into her mouth and he exhaled on a hiss of air. Wanting him every way a woman could take a man, she made love to him with her mouth, feeling him grow more swollen with each stroke of her tongue. She tasted the honey of his arousal.

He swore and pushed away, drawing her to her feet. His eyes black with passion, he shook his head. "I can't get enough of you."

Kissing each other, they climbed the stairs to her bedroom. He gently pushed her down on the bed and took a delicious journey with his mouth, starting with her throat then traveling to her breasts. All the while he rubbed her sweet spot, driving Nicola higher and higher.

Control burned away like mist on a hot summer morning. He replaced his hand with his mouth and his wicked tongue sent her over the edge.

She started to breathe again and he plunged inside her to the hilt. "Oh, wow," she managed, always amazed at the way he filled her completely.

"Oh, yeah," he said and began to pump inside her.

She looked into his eyes. His gaze held hers. She

couldn't have glanced away if she tried. In his eyes, she saw something that made mountains move and platelets shift. Her heart tripped over itself and the combination of emotion and physical sensation sent her over the edge again.

The following morning, he awakened earlier than she did. No surprise there, Nicola thought, stretching in the bed as she heard him climbing the steps. Abe was Mr. Early Riser. She'd had a hard time keeping up with his early schedule before she was pregnant. Now, when she often felt as if she needed more sleep, it would be even more difficult to win a morning race against him.

Wearing only his boxers, he entered her bedroom, carrying a cup of coffee for himself and a cup of tea for her. His hair was tousled from her hands, but his gaze was entirely too alert for first thing in the morning.

She smiled and sat up slowly, bringing the sheet with her. "Great room service."

He smiled in return. "I remember you've recently developed a preference for tea."

She took the cup. "Observant man. Thank you."

"You're welcome," he said, setting his coffee on the nightstand. He jostled the stand slightly. "Damn, my feet are too big for this room," he muttered. The cabinet door opened and Nicola's books spilled onto the carpet.

Alarm swept through her. She panicked, swearing under her breath and setting her tea on the other nightstand. Ditching her modesty, she scrambled across the bed to get to the books before he did. She didn't want him to see those books. She'd bought so many of them she'd had to cram them inside the cabinet before Abe arrived last night.

Her hand touched the first one at the same time his did.

He laughed. "Why the rush? Were you afraid I'd dump coffee on your books?"

"No, I just want to help," she said trying to shove them into the cabinet out of his sight. They slid back out.

"Hey, settle down. I'll get them." His large hands covered hers and she knew the second he read the title.

"What To Expect When You're Expecting?" he read aloud and she cringed. He glanced at the book underneath. *"Baby and Child Care. Successful Single Parenting."*

Abe looked at her then back at the books. He pinned her with a gaze that could melt steel. "There's only one reason I can think of that you would be reading these books."

Reaching blindly for the sheet, Nicola bit her lip. "I—uh—"

"How long have you known?" he demanded.

"Not that long," she said in a low voice. "My periods aren't particularly regular."

"I can't believe I didn't see this," he said, standing and still holding one of the books. "The stomach flu that lasted too long, the quick switch to tea and no wine," he said then narrowed his eyes. "But you drank wine last night?"

"It was water in a wineglass," she confessed, feeling silly. "I didn't want any questions."

"The baby's mine," he said, tossing the book on the bed and rubbing his forehead.

"Yes, it's yours, but you don't have to do anything." She took her heart in her hands. "I know you don't want any more children, but I have to have this child. I don't expect anything from you."

He rolled his eyes in disgust. "Nice try, Nic. Were you trying to get pregnant?"

She dropped her jaw in shock. "Absolutely not."

"You didn't make me use anything last night or the last time, either."

"That would have been trying to close the barn door after the horse got out," she said. "And why would I have been trying?"

"Some women use pregnancy as a way to snare a husband."

Guilt switched to anger in a nanosecond. "I think I've made it clear that I don't expect anything from you. If you don't recall, I repeatedly refused your offer to go to Washington and I tried several times to put our relationship on a professional footing." Fury raced through her. "I don't deserve this. Yes, I should have told you. But I couldn't figure out how, since you've made it abundantly clear you don't want any more children. I've spent the last few weeks torn apart over how to deal with this, how to keep this from hurting you or your career in any way."

"Too late for that, and we both know what the only solution is," he said, his jaw set like granite.

Her stomach twisted. "I'm not giving up the baby."

He swore. "I wasn't suggesting that. The only solution is for us to get married as soon as possible."

Abe felt as if he'd been caught with his pants down, literally. His mind went into crisis mode, developing a plan of action. "I know a judge who can push through the license so we won't have to wait. A civil ceremony will be the best route. We can get the blood tests from my doctor to assure discretion. I'll tell the kids about the baby after Christmas."

He glanced at her. She was looking at him as if he'd sprouted three heads. "There's no time to wait if you're already two months pregnant."

"I—I'm not sure it's a good idea to rush into marriage."

"This is an excellent reason to get married," he said. "I'm not having any more illegitimate children."

"We haven't even discussed marriage before," she returned, frowning.

"We would have eventually," he said and knew that the possibility, inevitability of marrying Nicola had been moving from the back of his mind to the forefront.

Her eyes full of doubt, she shook her head. "I'm not sure of that. We never discussed anything past Washington."

"Because you've been so difficult lately," he said. "If

you had allowed our relationship to develop naturally, then I'm sure we would have progressed to wanting something permanent."

"Naturally," she echoed. "Do you call this natural? 'Oh, Nicola, you're pregnant. We're getting married this afternoon.'"

"We don't have time to allow things to develop naturally now. We have to do this for our child. We'll work out our relationship after we take care of the legalities." He reached down and gave her a quick, firm kiss. "I have to get moving. Harold and Miranda won't mind being witnesses. Let's shoot for four o'clock."

"Abe, I'm not easy about this."

"I'll make it easy," he promised. He would take care of the fear and doubt in her eyes.

By four o'clock that afternoon, he had a judge, witnesses in the form of Harold, Miranda, Abe's daughter Kimberly and the new love of her life, Navy SEAL Zach. Kimberly and Zach had shown up early for Christmas. Abe had demanded and received expedited results of the blood tests and sent a driver to pick up Nicola.

At five minutes after, he wondered if the driver had run into traffic. He pushed out the cell number for the chauffeur. "Henry, where are you?"

"Uh, I'm still in Miss Granville's driveway, sir. She told me she won't need the car. She told me I can wait till Christmas, but she's not coming."

Shock rendered him speechless. He felt the gazes of everyone in the room on him. "She said what?"

"She said she's not coming."

"Thanks, Henry," he said in a voice that sounded clipped to his own ears. "Keep the motor running." He punched out Nicola's number. "Henry says there's been a misunderstanding about the time of your arrival."

He heard her sigh on the phone. "I'm really not comfortable with this."

"Nicola, we don't have time for this. It's the right thing to do."

"Not for me," she said, her voice shaking. "Not right now."

"Nic," he said. "Nic—" He glanced at his phone and got the *Call Lost* message. The woman had not only stood him up at the altar, she'd hung up on him.

Twelve

"**A**be?" his brother, Harold, said.

Abe shook his head in disbelief. "She's not coming."

Judge Kilgore cleared his throat. "Then I assume you won't be needing me this afternoon," he said. "You have my number if there's a change. If you'll excuse me," the man said and left the room.

His daughter Kimberly moved closer. "This has happened pretty fast. Maybe Nicola just needs a little time."

"Exactly," Harold's wife, Miranda, said. "You've barely given the poor woman time to breathe and a woman's emotions during pregnancy can be a tricky thing."

"Hear, hear, to that," Harold said.

"Pregnancy," Kimberly echoed and looked at her father in disbelief. "You got Nicola pregnant?"

His gorgeous, brainy twenty-five-year-old daughter Kimberly was known for her bluntness. She claimed it was the only way she'd been able to hold her own with her brothers. "Yes, she's pregnant. Yes, I'm the father."

"But you're too old for that," she said.

Harold chuckled. "Apparently not."

Abe threw a sharp glance at both of them. "I don't have time to explain. I have to figure out how to get through to Nicola. I told her I would take care of all the arrangements. The ceremony would be at 4:00 p.m." His head spinning, he began to pace. Why had she backed out?

"You *told* her you were going to get married?" Kimberly asked.

"It was the only course of action. She's apparently been pregnant for two months. It had to be expedited," he said firmly.

"Gosh, how romantic," Kim said sarcastically. "Did you give her the orders in military time, too?"

· Her new husband, Zach, put his hand on her shoulder to calm her. "Honey, you don't need to hammer the guy. He's just trying to do the right thing."

"But you can't order someone to marry you," she argued. "And Nicola's more girly than I am. She might have wanted a church wedding with a dress and a reception."

"You could have at least let her get a dress," Harold's wife scolded.

Abe had a sinking feeling in his gut. "I thought," he said and corrected himself. "I knew it was best to do this as soon as possible."

"I still can't believe you knocked up your campaign manager," Kim said, shaking her head.

Abe noticed Zach give his daughter a jab in the ribs. "She's not knocked up. She's pregnant with my child."

"And her child," Kim pointed out.

"That's what I said."

"No, you said your child. I realize you have control issues, but not everyone likes someone else to make major life decisions for them." She glanced at Zach and her gaze softened. "Although some of your interfering decisions turn out well, some of us get a little testy about being told what to do. Here's a news flash, Dad. Some women like to be asked."

"My daughter seems to have grown more assertive since she got involved with you," Abe muttered to Zach.

"She said it has to do with confidence, sir," Zach said.

Abe nodded absently, his head spinning with ways to fix this predicament. "So I should ask her," he murmured to himself. "She doesn't trust me yet," he said. "I would trust her with my life, but she doesn't trust me yet."

The room went completely quiet.

"You're really in love with her," Kimberly said, astonished. "You're messed up about this. I've never seen you this way." She put her hand on his arm and he felt her searching gaze. "You really love her, don't you?"

He nodded, his gut burning at the same time a weight felt as if it was lifted from his chest. "Yeah, I do."

"Have you told her?" Kimberly asked.

It took Abe an hour to figure out where he'd gone wrong and what he needed to do to correct it. In the meantime, he told the driver he could return to Crofthaven and Abe took some antacid, changed out of his suit and headed over to Nicola's.

He rang the doorbell four times before she answered. Her eyes were red from crying. He felt like pond scum.

"Oh, sweetheart, I'm sorry," he said, stepping inside and pulling her into his arms.

"I couldn't do it, Abe. It just felt so wrong. We're not ready for marriage."

"I disagree from my side, but if you need time, you can have it, Nicola."

She glanced up at him with a searching gaze.

"I handled this all wrong. I shouldn't have ordered you to marry me. Miranda can't believe I didn't let you at least get a dress. I should have asked. I should have told you that I love you and I need you in my life, forever. And it's kinda late now, isn't it?"

She nodded sadly.

"Hard to believe how much I could screw this up."

She took a careful breath. "I think you were trying to protect the baby."

"And you, too," he said. "I still want you to marry me.

I would have bought a ring, but I don't know your taste and I'd like you to be part of that choice if you decide you can put up with me for the rest of my life. I couldn't believe it when you didn't show up for the wedding. It hit me hard, but not having you in my life at all would hit me a lot harder. So, if you need time, you've got it. Just give us a chance."

She gave a little shudder and tears streamed down her cheeks. "But there are things you don't know about me. Things you may not be able to accept about me."

"Tell me," he said. "Try me."

She shuddered again and looked away. "Oh, this is hard. I was pregnant before, when I was a teenager," she said, her voice barely a whisper. "I gave up the baby for adoption."

Shock, followed quickly by compassion rushed through him. His heart wrenched for her. Remembering that she'd told him about her high school boyfriend bailing on her, he pulled her against him again. "Oh, Nic, you poor thing, having to go through all that by yourself. No mother, no father around."

"I felt so guilty," she said, sniffing. "I still feel guilty. Like I should have done more to keep her, but I had no money, no family." Her voice broke.

"Have you ever checked on her?"

She nodded. "I get photos every year from the adoptive family. She's doing great. She has a wonderful family. She hasn't asked to meet me, though, and unless she does, I think it's right that I stay away." She took a shaky breath. "This is part of the reason I couldn't marry you, Abe. I didn't know if you could accept it."

Looking into her pain-filled eyes, Abe knew he had never felt so much love for another person in his life. "Accept that you got into a rough situation and made the best decision for someone other than yourself? Accept that you did your best for your baby? How could I not love you even more for that?"

Her eyes filled with tears again. "Oh, Abe."

"Nic," he said, holding her precious face in his hands. "I obviously haven't made it clear to you how much you mean to me, how much better my life is since you came into it. I love you and I will love our child. Don't you understand? If you marry me, you're giving me a chance to get it all right this time."

On the day before Christmas Eve, Nicola gave Abe the chance of a lifetime he was asking for by saying, "I do."

"I now pronounce you man and wife," the judge said, and Nicola tilted her head upward for Abe's kiss of commitment.

At Miranda's urging, Nicola wore a new dress suit for the occasion. The waist was a little tight and she suspected that due to her baby's growth, she wouldn't be wearing it again for several months. She looked into Abe's eyes and saw the light of love. It was still hard to believe. He'd done a complete turnaround on the baby and he was as randy as ever for Nicola morning, noon and night.

"I love you," she said.

"I love you," he echoed, and she felt his declaration vibrate in every fiber inside her.

Kimberly wiped her eyes and embraced her father. "Congratulations, Dad!"

Lea rushed to Nicola's side. "Congratulations, Nicola."

"Welcome to the family," Reid said. "You've already done wonders," he whispered to Nicola. "The love of a good woman can make miracles happen."

Five months later, Nicola lay in the bed of the Georgetown home she shared with Abe and his children and nieces and nephews when they got a chance to visit. Her nightgown pushed up just below her breasts, she tried not to laugh as Abe sang an off-key rendition of "Eensy Weensy Spider" with his mouth pressed against her belly.

He finished slaughtering the children's song and kissed her belly. "How was that?"

"Horrible, and you know it," she said. "You're great in many ways, but vocal performance isn't your forte. We're supposed to be playing Mozart for the baby."

"Bull," Abe said. "Mozart isn't going to pay for my child's education. Mozart isn't going to get up for middle of the night feedings. Mozart isn't going to change messy diapers."

"And you are?" she asked, lifting her eyebrows.

He lifted his hand as if he was making an oath. "On my honor, I will get up for middle of the night feedings and change messy diapers. But not all of them," he added and rolled to her side. He caressed her belly with his hand. "As long as I get you all to myself sometimes."

Her heart fluttered at the seductive expression in his eyes. It amazed her that he could want her so much when her body seemed huge. "I like it when you get me all to yourself."

"Good," he said, moving his hand up to cup her breast. "I love your body."

She shook her head. "I look like a beached whale."

He shook his head. "No, you remind me of a ripe juicy peach that I want to devour every day." He took her mouth in a kiss. "Are you too tired tonight?"

She shook her head. "No." Feeling her body heat in anticipation, she nuzzled his chest. "You have a wonderful way of making me forget I'm tired."

"I'm so lucky," he said. "So lucky. To have you as my wife, to give me a child." He kissed her. "And to give me back the children I felt like I'd lost."

Nicola pinched herself for the millionth time. Abe had given her love and a family. Everything she'd wanted but never had, he'd given her.

"Are you pinching yourself again?" he asked.

She smiled and laughed. "Yes."

"No pinching allowed," he told her. "I've got better things in mind for your body."

Better was an understatement.

* * * * *

*The Dynasty series continues next month
with a brand-new family.
Set in the glamorous world of wine-making,*
DYNASTIES: THE ASHTONS,
*introduces you to a very convoluted family
where blood is not always thicker than wine.*

Look for the excitement to begin with
ENTANGLED
by Eileen Wilks,
available January.

Silhouette® Desire®

**A compelling new family saga begins
as scandals from the past bring turmoil to
the lives of the Ashtons of Napa Valley, in**

ENTANGLED
by Eileen Wilks
(Silhouette Desire #1627)

For Cole Ashton, his family vineyard was his first priority,
until sexy Dixie McCord walked back into his life, reminding
him of their secret affair he'd been unable to forget.
Determined to get her out of his system once and for all, Cole
planned a skillful seduction. What he didn't plan was that
he'd fall for Dixie even harder than he had the first time!

DYNASTIES: THE ASHTONS

**A family built on lies...
brought together by dark, passionate secrets.**

Available at your favorite retail outlet.

introduces an exciting new family saga
with

DYNASTIES : THE DANFORTHS

A family of prominence...
tested by scandal, sustained by passion!

Silhouette

Desire.

Coming in January 2005

BETWEEN MIDNIGHT AND MORNING
by Cindy Gerard
Silhouette Desire #1630

Small-town veterinarian Alison Samuels hardly
expected to start a fiery affair with hunky young
rancher John Tyler. To John, she was a stimulating
challenge, and Alison was more than game.
But he hid a dark past, and Alison wasn't
one for surprises....

*Available wherever
Silhouette books
are sold.*

COMING NEXT MONTH

#1627 ENTANGLED—Eileen Wilks
Dynasties: The Ashtons
Years ago, Cole Ashton and Dixie McCord's passionate affair had ended when Cole's struggling business had taken priority over Dixie. Now, she was back in his life and Cole hoped for a second chance. But even if he could win Dixie once more, would Cole be able to make the right choice this time?

#1628 HER PASSIONATE PLAN B—Dixie Browning
Divas Who Dish
Spunky nurse Daisy Hunter never thought she'd find the man of her dreams while on the job! But when a patient's relative, athlete Kell McGee, arrived in town, she suddenly had to make a difficult decision—stick to her old agenda for finding a man or switch to passionate Plan B!

#1629 THE FIERCE AND TENDER SHEIKH—Alexandra Sellers
Sons of the Desert
Sheikh Sharif found long-lost Princess Shakira fifteen years after she'd escaped her family's assassination. As the beautiful princess helped heal her homeland, Sharif passionately worked on mending Shakira's spirit. Though years as a refugee had left her hardened, could the fierce and tender sheikh provide the heat needed to melt Shakira's cool facade and expose her heart?

#1630 BETWEEN MIDNIGHT AND MORNING—Cindy Gerard
When veterinarian Alison Samuels moved into middle-of-nowhere Montana, she hardly expected to start a fiery affair, especially with hunky young rancher John Tyler. To J.T., this tantalizing older woman was a stimulating challenge and Alison was more than game. But J.T. hid a dark past and Alison wasn't one for surprises....

#1631 IN FORBIDDEN TERRITORY—Shawna Delacorte
Playboy Tyler Farrel was totally taken when he laid eyes on the breathtakingly beautiful Angie Coleman. She was all grown up! Despite their mutual attraction, Ty wouldn't risk seducing his best friend's kid sister until Angie, sick of being overprotected, decided to step into forbidden territory.

#1632 BUSINESS AFFAIRS—Shirley Rogers
When Jenn Cardon placed the highest bid at a bachelor auction, she had no idea she'd just landed a romantic getaway with sexy blue-eyed CEO Alex Dunnigan—her boss! Thanks to cozy quarters, sexual tension turned into unbridled passion. Alex wasn't into commitment but Jenn had a secret that could keep him around...forever.

SDCNM1204